IT HAPPENED ON A HOLIDAY

by Lavinia R. Davis

Lavinia R. Davis

IT HAPPENED
ON A HOLIDAY

ILLUSTRATED BY JEAN MACDONALD PORTER

DOUBLEDAY & CO., INC.

GARDEN CITY, NEW YORK,

1958.

CONTENTS

IT HAPPENED ON A HOLIDAY

NEW YEAR'S RESCUE

All during the late summer and early fall the good Brothers of the order of St. Bernard worked to get ready for the winter. They grew and harvested food, cut wood for fuel, brought in medical supplies, and trained their wonderful dogs. The hospice, which was a home, a church, and shelter for travelers, hung like a great bird's nest high up in the Swiss Alps near the narrow footpath which led from Germany to Italy. With the coming of cold weather and heavy snow the Brothers would have no time for anything but helping people who were lost or who had fallen and hurt themselves trying to cross over the mountains. So they spent their summers and early autumns getting ready for the long, cold winters.

Now on one frosty morning long ago Brother John and Brother Charles stood just outside the hospice gate watching four young dogs which Brother John had been training. Brother John whistled and instantly three of the dogs wheeled and ran toward him. The fourth dog only looked at Brother John and began to prance about just out of his reach. "A foolish disobedient creature that one," Brother Charles said and Brother John whistled louder than ever. This time the dog came forward with such a rush that he knocked Brother Charles down in the process.

"The stupid clumsy brute!" Brother Charles sputtered. "Not worth the food we've been feeding him."

"Oh, he means well," Brother John said. Brother John's voice shook a little because Brother Charles was in charge of supplies for the hospice and if he took a dislike to a dog, it was apt to go hungry. "He's just a little too playful."

"Bah. Rubbish! Fiddlesticks!" Brother Charles said, because now the silly dog was trying to lick his face and he didn't like it. "That silly cur is an insult to dogdom and the order of St. Bernard. It is hard to believe that he is the same kind of animal as the wonderful Barry who saved forty human beings from death in the snow and lost his own life saving the forty-first!"

"But Barry was older and wiser than this dog when he made all those rescues," Brother John said gently.

"This foolish one is little more than a puppy. Why, he won't be a year old until New Year's Day."

"He'll never live to see the New Year, if I can help it," Brother Charles answered. "In fact I doubt if the abbot will keep him after tomorrow. With food and fuel so hard to come by we can't waste it on such a stupid useless creature."

With that Brother Charles hurried off to speak to the abbot who was the head of the hospice. Meanwhile Brother John, who loved all the dogs, even this stupid and disobedient one, went on patiently schooling and teaching. Usually Brother John enjoyed his work but right now he was too worried to enjoy anything. He knew that the very next day the abbot planned to give the four young dogs their grown-up names and their St. Bernard collars. The collars were made of good leather and there was a small keg of brandy fastened to each one to warm up any half-frozen men the dogs might find in the mountains. No dog was ever named or given a St. Bernard collar until he was obedient, well behaved, and trained in rescue work. So the next day, which was a sort of dog's baptism and graduation combined, was terribly important. Yet here was this one foolish pup who hadn't learned any of his lessons.

Right now while the other three dogs went through their paces all over again the fourth dog lay down well out of Brother John's reach and wagged his tail.

He didn't even look like the other St. Bernard dogs, much less act like them. He was larger and shaggier than the others and his coat was spattered with black and white patches. His broad clumsy paws looked too big for the rest of him and his light-colored eyes always seemed to be laughing. Usually when Brother John looked at the dog he felt like laughing too, but today when he thought of what was likely to happen to the poor foolish creature he sighed instead.

As soon as Brother John sighed the big shaggy dog pranced over to cheer him up. The dog's head was cocked to one side so that his patches looked like a party hat. The white fur on his oversized paws looked like thick woolen socks. As the dog rolled over and over in front of Brother John, the good man had to smile in spite of his worries. He smiled and reached out to pat the dog and hoped with all his heart that tomorrow at the name-giving the silly creature would behave himself.

But the next day nothing happened the way Brother John had hoped that it would. Right after early prayers the abbot, the Brothers, the older dogs, and three of the young ones went out to the hospice yard for the naming. Every living creature was there— EXCEPT—the foolish dog with the black and white patches.

Brother John whistled. Instantly the dog bounded out of the hospice and pranced toward him. The

4

dog's head was held high. His tail wagged proudly. And in his big, foolish mouth was a boot. It was a new boot. A good leather boot. It belonged to the abbot who was head of the hospice!

"Foolish One. Silly. Put that back!" Brother John whispered. The dog looked surprised. He dropped the boot at Brother John's feet and rolled over, playing dead. "Clown. Idiot," Brother John scolded. "Put it back!"

The foolish dog thumped his tail against the ground. He crawled on his stomach and licked Brother John's toes so it tickled. But he didn't put the boot back. Brother John had to do that himself.

The abbot said nothing and went on with the ceremony. He gave each of the three well-behaved dogs a collar and blessed it. He named them Royal and Duke and Trusty. Then he turned to the fourth dog and frowned so that Brother John shook with fright as to what might happen. "That is the dog, I told you about, Reverend Father,"said Brother Charles. "The cur who does nothing but eat and play foolish pranks like the one we have all just witnessed. Surely with winter upon us we need not keep such a hungry useless creature."

"But, Reverend Father, the dog means well," Brother John began, and held onto the dog so he couldn't jump up on the abbot. "As I told Brother Charles, he will not be a year old until New Year's."

"And that's two months off and think of all the food he will eat in the meantime," Brother Charles said crossly. "Not to mention all the other trouble he'll bring to the hospice. Shoot him now and be done with it."

"No. No. Give him another chance!" Brother John pleaded, and the words had a queer choked sound because he cared so much and besides the dog was licking his face, which made talking difficult. "Please. I'll share my own food with him."

The abbot looked at the dog for a long, long moment. Then he shrugged his shoulders and turned to Brother John. "Very well," he said. "You may keep him, but only until the New Year. Unless he has learned to behave and be useful by New Year's Day he must die, and you, Brother John, as his teacher and trainer, are the one who will have to get rid of him."

Of course after that Brother John didn't dare ask the abbot for the foolish dog's collar or mention that he still hadn't been given a grown-up dog's name. As for the other Brothers they just called the dog, "Stupid" or "Clumsy" and when he was especially bad they shouted, "Stop that, you FOOL."

In fact, except for Brother John nobody paid much attention to the foolish dog at all. Brother John went on working with him, and praying for him, and saw to it that he had his fair share of food and a place near the fire even when it meant going hungry and cold himself. But as the days of the old year grew shorter and fewer, even Brother John was discouraged.

"Heaven help you, Foolish One," Brother John said, and patted the big shaggy head. "Unless a Christmas miracle brings some sense to that head of yours, I'll never be allowed to keep you."

But Christmas time came and went and nothing happened except that out of doors the cold grew worse and inside the hospice there was less food than ever for the men and dogs who worked there. The snow fell and fell and on many mountain paths there were drifts as high and higher than a tall man's head. All during Christmas week the good Brothers of St. Bernard worked hard trying to give food and warmth and shelter to helpless strangers who passed their door. And by day and by night, often without taking time off for food and rest, the men and their dogs fought their way through the snow to rescue travelers who were lost in the mountains.

The dogs went out in teams of three. When they found a man lying hurt and helpless in the deep snow one dog crouched on either side of him. This way they kept off the wind and warmed him with their own animal warmth. At the same time the third dog went back to the hospice. From there he brought the Brothers to help the poor traveler back to warmth and safety.

7

On New Year's Eve the worst storm of all raged over the mountains. The long night was a torment and a misery at the hospice. Brother Charles and the abbot himself were in bed with a fever. All the dogs were half starved and two of the best of them were dead, lost in a blizzard of ten days earlier.

Late at night Brother John sat by a failing fire, with only the foolish dog for company. The silly thing lay on its back waving its big paws in the air, for all the world like a circus dog. But for once Brother John could not laugh at such clowning. There were tears in his eyes because he knew that in the morning the Foolish One must die and there was nothing he could say or do to save him. With food and firewood so scarce that men died from cold and starvation the Brothers could not keep a great hungry beast who did nothing but play.

At that moment Brother John heard a sound above the noise of the wind outside. He pushed open the door and at first the driving snow blinded him. Then he saw Trusty. The faithful dog fell at his feet, half dead with the cold. Brother John pulled him inside and covered him with his own blanket.

He knew that Trusty had gone out with Duke and Royal and that now those two crouched at the side of some lost traveler. Trusty had fought his way through the storm to the hospice for help. But now there was no strength left in him to guide a man back to where help was needed.

Brother John pulled on his cloak and reached for a lantern. If he went at once, before more snow filled up Trusty's paw marks, he might be able to find the way. He went out of the door and the shaggy dog bounced out ahead of him. "Come back. Come back at once!" Brother John shouted, but the wind blew the words back in his throat, and besides the dog seldom minded even when he could hear.

The good man bent his head and pushed on step by step. There was no way to catch the Foolish One and perhaps it was just as well. Better to have him lost in the storm than to die tomorrow at the hands of a man he had thought was his friend.

Brother John had only gone a few feet before he saw that Trusty's paw marks were already covered over by the driving snow. He prayed silently and forced himself forward against the biting wind. One step. Two steps.

Brother John shook with cold as he tried to decide which way to go. Everywhere he looked there was snow and ice. How could he tell where to turn with no paw marks to guide him? What was to keep him from tumbling into an abyss and crashing to his death? How could he tell where the snow lay deepest and where there might be a chance of going ahead?

Suddenly a strange thing happened. A big shaggy

body came up beside him, pushing him forward and shielding him from the wind. It was the stupid dog, of course, the idiot, the Foolish One. Brother John gripped the dog's shaggy fur and they walked on together into the storm.

In spite of the wind and the snow and the bitter cold they went on step by step, up into the mountains. Brother John's body grew numb, and his feet were like lead. Only his own courage and the great strength of the overgrown dog kept him from falling.

At last he saw a small flicker of light. It was a traveler's lantern. Beyond it, sheltered by peaks of snow-covered rock, were Royal and Duke on either side of a man's still body. As Brother John looked down at the man, he thought he was already dead. He crossed himself and prayed and would have turned away, but the dog blocked his path. The foolish creature barked and clowned and pulled at Brother John's cloak with his teeth.

For once Brother John was angry. "Fool! Idiot!" he said. "Must you clown even in the face of death?"

But the dog kept up his silly antics and at last Brother John understood what was wanted. He turned then and tugged the traveler's body across the dog's broad back. Once more the dog barked, and this time Royal and Duke understood him too. Royal took the lead. Duke moved beside Brother John, shielding him from the wind. The Foolish One with his heavy load

came last of all. And so they traveled down the mountain and back through the storm.

At last they saw lights in the hospice window. The abbot himself opened the door to them. He and Brother Charles lifted the traveler from the dog's back and tended him gently. Trusty feebly wagged his tail in a welcome.

But Brother John had eyes and ears for nothing but the foolish dog who lay, scarcely breathing, at his feet. Would the dog live or had the terrible journey been too much for him? And if he lived through the night, what was in store for him tomorrow?

Across the room the traveler stirred. "Your dogs," he whispered. "Your wonderful dogs have saved my life."

The abbot put a blanket around Brother John's shaking shoulders and asked for the whole story of the rescue. Brother John told him everything, even to how the big dog had barked and clowned at the top of the mountain.

"Your Foolish One has earned his place with us," the abbot said when he had heard the story. "And earned it royally by making the first rescue of the New Year. In the morning Brother John, we shall give him his St. Bernard collar and any name you like."

"Barry! Barry the second!" Brother John said and then remembering how the foolish dog had knocked over Brother Charles and stolen the abbot's boot, he spoke more slowly. "If he lives, Reverend Father, can I name him Barry after the greatest of all St. Bernards?"

"He will live, my son," the abbot said and smiled as the dog stirred and began feebly licking Brother John's hand. "And the name is well chosen."

Brother Charles said nothing, and as he tottered off to the kitchen Brother John was afraid that he was still angry. A little while later he came back with two bowls of hot nourishing soup. "This is for you Brother John," he said. "And this is for Barry, the second. The old year in which the dog and I were so foolish is over and the New Year well begun."

THE HAPPY VALENTINE

It was Valentine's Day and the school bus had just stopped in front of the MacKay house. Jimmy MacKay got off the school bus and hurried home. Jimmy was in such a rush he almost dropped his valentines in a February mud puddle in the middle of the front lawn. Jimmy almost dropped his valentines, but not quite. Somehow he caught them and raced indoors and up to his own room.

Then Jimmy put the valentines he had made at school in a little pile together. Next he put the valentines that the other children and Miss Blake, the second-grade teacher, had given him all around his room. They looked just beautiful, but Jimmy didn't waste a single minute looking at them. Instead he took out the valentine he had made for Grandma

MacKay and covered it very carefully with his biggest picture books. Today was Grandma MacKay's birthday as well as Valentine's Day. So of course Jimmy wanted to make specially sure that nothing happened to her valentine before he gave it to her at suppertime.

When Jimmy had finished with the valentines he emptied his piggy bank into his pocket. Then he hurried downstairs again to see Grandma. Grandma MacKay sat in the living-room rocking chair with baby Betty in her arms. Grandma rocked gently back and forth and all the time she sang and talked to baby Betty. Grandma and baby Betty were so happy and so busy they didn't think of anything but each other. But Jimmy MacKay, who was seven, did think about something else. He thought about the present he wanted to give Grandma MacKay for her birthday.

"Grandma," said Jimmy, and he jingled the ten pennies in his pocket, "what do you like best in the world?"

"New things," said Grandma and smiled down at baby Betty. "Live things and pretty things. All things that are soft and sweet and happy."

Jimmy didn't say a word. He put his hand deep in his pocket, jingled his ten pennies, and went outside. Then he walked down the country road to the village store. As he walked he thought about what Grandma MacKay had said and about the present he would buy for her.

When Jimmy was at the village store he looked over all the things that cost ten pennies. He looked at pads and at pencils. He looked at animal crackers and at lollipops. He even looked at hairpins and handkerchiefs. Now all of these things were new. Too, the animal crackers and the lollipops, were sweet. And the handkerchief was soft and pretty. But there was nothing in the village store, even for ten times ten pennies, that was all of these things, and alive and happy as well.

Just then Mr. Cork, who ran the village store, came over to talk to Jimmy. "I have ten cents to spend," Jimmy said, and showed Mr. Cork his pennies. "For a valentine-birthday present."

"That ought to be a very special present then," Mr. Cork said and pointed to some fine new kites that were marked .25¢ each. "A valentine-birthday present is so special that I'll let you have one of these fine new kites for ten cents instead of for a quarter of a dollar."

Jimmy shook his head. Before he could tell Mr. Cork that the present was for Grandma MacKay, Mr. Cork led him over to the door and pointed outside. There were some boys flying kites outside the store. The kites were exactly like the ones Mr. Cork had just shown to Jimmy. Only these kites were flying way up in the sky. They were so high up that they looked alive and so pretty that it made Jimmy happy just to look at them. It made Jimmy feel happy all over to watch the kites until he remembered Grandma Mac-Kay's present. Then he didn't feel happy a bit. He felt pulled this way and that way at the same time. First Jimmy felt pulled right back toward the kite counter inside the store. Second Jimmy felt pulled away from Mr. Cork's store before he could spend his pennies on anything but Grandma MacKay's present.

The second pull won. Jimmy hurried out of Mr. Cork's store so fast that the pennies jingled louder than ever in his pocket. By this time the jingling of the pennies didn't sound cheerful to Jimmy. It only meant that he hadn't been able to find Grandma MacKay a present that was any of the things that she wanted.

Jimmy walked slowly home along the country road. He walked so slowly that now the pennies in his pocket didn't jingle at all. Jimmy didn't care. He was too tired and sad to care. He was tired from his long walk and from being pulled this way and that about the kite. And of course he was sad because now it was too late to buy Grandma MacKay a present.

When Jimmy was very nearly home he heard a bird. The bird was a chickadee and it sang such a quick, gay little song that Jimmy stopped to listen. He looked around and saw the bird sitting in some bushes. Jimmy went closer and the bird flew off, but just then Jimmy saw something else on those bushes.

Jimmy saw something gray and pretty. He put his hand out to feel and it was soft and sweet to the touch. It was a pussy willow! A new, pretty pussy willow that hadn't been there last week. Jimmy took out his knife and began to cut very carefully. By the time he had cut a nice bunch he forgot that he had ever been tired or sad. Now he was so thrilled and excited that he ran all the way home.

The pussy willows were new, the pussy willows were alive and soft and pretty. Jimmy was sure they were all the things that Grandma had said except happy. Jimmy wasn't sure about that, which was why he ran as fast as he could go to find out!

As soon as Jimmy reached home he hurried upstairs. He got all clean and scrubbed for supper without anyone telling him. Then he picked up the valentines he had made at school and the one he had made at home for Grandma. He carried the valentines in his right hand and the pussy willows in his left hand and went to the dining room. He had just put Grandma MacKay's pussy willows and her valentine down at her place when Mother called everybody in to supper.

"Grandma, look!" Jimmy said, and now he just couldn't wait to know if the pussy willows were all the things that Grandma liked the best. "They're for you. For your birthday."

Grandma looked at the pussy willows and opened the valentine. "Thank you, Jimmy!" she said. "Thank you. You couldn't have given me anything that would make me as happy as pussy willows."

When Jimmy heard that he laughed so that baby Betty who was in her pen looked up at him and laughed too. "You like new things," Jimmy said, "live things and pretty things, and all things that are soft and sweet and happy. That means baby Betty and pussy willows, doesn't it, Grandma?"

"That's right," Grandma said and she gave Jimmy a smile that made him feel proud and happy and thrilled all over. "But I don't like them any better than fine, strong, thoughtful, generous ones, just like my grandson Jimmy."

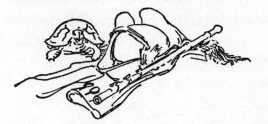

A TURTLE, A FLUTE, AND THE GENERAL'S BIRTHDAY

Ludwig von Bram reached for his flute while he was still sound asleep. His fingers gripped the smoothly polished wood through the straw of his bedding and he settled back with a blissful sigh. Ludwig was having a perfectly wonderful dream. He dreamed that he was playing his flute to General and Mrs. Washington and all the general's aides and other officers.

By day, Ludwig, who was twelve, worked as the cook's boy and was the youngest and least important person in all of Valley Forge. At night he pretended he was a flute player in one of the bands of the Continental Army. This was what Grandfather von Zarn had expected him to be when Ludwig had joined the army in the fall of 1777. "Take care of my flute,"

Grandpa von Zarn had said. "And see to it you be-have like a soldier and a musician. Remember every-thing I've taught you about military bands."

"I will. I will," Ludwig had said, but he hadn't known what was ahead of him in the cold miserable months at Valley Forge. He was set to work at once hauling water and wood and scouring pots without even a chance of listening to band music. The only part of his promise he was able to keep was to take care of the flute, which he never let out of his sight.

At that moment one of the twelve soldiers with whom Ludwig shared a drafty newly built hut nudged him with the toe of a cracked boot. "Time to get up, boy," the soldier said. "Nearly daybreak."

For an instant Ludwig only gripped his precious flute tighter than ever and tried to dig himself deeper into the straw which served as both mattress and blanket. Then he remembered that today, Febru-ary 22, was General Washington's birthday, and jumped to his feet. Since he slept in his clothes, he only had to fasten his flute to the string he used for a belt before he hurried off toward the headquarters cookhouse.

As Ludwig ran down the wagon-rutted road, he hoped against hope he would not be late. Master Bridgeman, the headquarters cook, was not an easy man to work for at the best of times. The long hard months with little fuel and less food had not improved his temper. Then recently, when Mrs. Washington joined her husband in the field-stone farmhouse which served as headquarters, Master Bridgeman drove Ludwig and his two grown-up helpers frantic with orders and commands. Master Bridgeman moaned and groaned over the lack of decent provisions with which to cook dinner. He huffed and puffed like the bellows he used for the fire. Yesterday, when he had learned that the Fourth Artillery planned to serenade the general in honor of his birthday, was the worst of all. "If the general is to have music he shall have enough to eat," the cook had roared. "I, Peter Bridgeman, first-class chef, shall see to it if I have to use young Ludwig here in the soup pot."

Ludwig knew that was a joke, but there was nothing funny about the tone of Master Bridgeman's voice or his beatings, so right now he ran as fast as he could go. The sun was barely up by the time he reached the hut which served as dining hall and kitchen, but even so Master Bridgeman and Privates Lanky and Scopes were ahead of him. "Slugabed!" Master Bridgeman handed Ludwig a wooden bucket. "Fill this at the well and come back on the double. There's work to be done!"

Ludwig couldn't think of a day during the cold miserable months he had been at Valley Forge when there hadn't been work to do, but this once he almost enjoyed it. After all that General Washington had done for his troops it was a privilege to do anything, no matter how hard and dull, which might help to make his birthday party a success. For the next few hours Ludwig carried water and wood and raked up ashes in the big open fireplace where Master Bridgeman did his cooking. As Ludwig worked he wished that he could play his flute for the general the way he had in his dream. But of course now with Master Bridgeman watching him he didn't even dare put the instrument to his lips.

For the next few hours Master Bridgeman kept everyone jumping. Then at nine o'clock he sent for a wagon and he and the two privates started to drive over to the quartermaster's after supplies for the birthday dinner. "As for you boy, see that you keep busy," Master Bridgeman warned Ludwig. "The pots and the spit are to be cleaned, the ashes raked, and the fire tended. No daydreaming now nor playing on that flute if you know what's good for you."

Ludwig meant to keep on working but after he had cleaned the big black pots and the spit he was so hungry and tired he simply had to rest. He cleaned his hands and ate a heel of bread. That made him feel so much better that without really knowing what he was doing he untied the flute at his side and began to play. I'll only play for a moment, he thought. Just for a minute or two before I fetch more wood for the fire.

So Ludwig began to play, and soon he forgot everything but his music. He forgot the ashes he was to rake and the wood he was to put on the fire. After a while the fire went out, but Ludwig didn't notice it. He was so wrapped up in his playing that he didn't hear the supply wagon creak to a stop outside the hut or see Master Bridgeman hurry through the door.

The first thing Ludwig knew the cook was beside him boxing his ears until Ludwig saw stars. "So!" Master Bridgeman sputtered. "So you let the fire go out while my back was turned. It is not enough that I am asked to prepare dinner for General Washington without decent supplies to cook with. No, I must also be cursed with a good-for-nothing flute player to work in my kitchen. Give me that flute, you lazy young rascal. I have half a mind to use it for kindling."

"No. No!" Ludwig shrank back against the rough wall of the hut. "Don't take the flute."

Just then Private Scopes and Private Lanky came in and Master Bridgeman told them what had happened. "It would serve the boy right if I beat him black and blue with his own flute," he said, "and then used it for kindling. When we have just been cheated out of the provisions we were promised for tonight, this is too much!"

Private Lanky shrugged and gave Ludwig a push

toward the open door. "Send the lad off to find food or kindling," he said and gave Ludwig another push that looked rough but wasn't. "After all, he might snare a bird or find some pine boughs to keep out drafts." With that he gave Ludwig still another push and whispered the word "Run!" so that only Ludwig could hear him.

Ludwig ran. He ran as fast as he could but even so he could hear Master Bridgeman shouting out all the terrible things that would happen to him if he came back empty-handed. Ludwig ran until he had to stop for breath and then he walked and ran again. He went up hill and down dale, past the huts of the Maryland Rifles, the Second Virginia Regiment, Colonel Morgan's men, and on to the last outpost of the camp. Wherever he looked the country was bare and bleak in the thin February sunshine. Every tree and every branch for miles around had been used up long ago. As for birds, there wasn't so much as a chickadee in sight.

By the time Ludwig reached a little valley near an S-shaped pond he simply had to sit down on a rock to rest. "Run," Private Lanky had said. "Run." Did the private mean run away, desert, and take his chances of getting home to Pottstown without being caught? Ludwig fingered his flute as he always did when he was thinking. Then he started to play the old, brave tunes which he had learned from his grandfather who had played in a royal military band in Bavaria. Finally he switched to "Yankee Doodle" and by that time he knew he couldn't run away and be a deserter, no matter what happened. He'd simply have to find a way to hide his flute and go back and take whatever beatings Master Bridgeman chose to give him. It wouldn't be easy. Ludwig shivered as he thought of it. He could almost feel the sickening thud and cut of Master Bridgeman's wide belt on his own bare back. It wouldn't be easy at all and especially not when he couldn't play his flute to give him courage. Better enjoy as much of it as he could right now, and then perhaps he would be able to hear the sound of it in his memory when he needed it most.

Ludwig played and played and once more he forgot where he was and everything about him. He didn't even see the tall young man in the shabby artillery uniform who came toward him around the curving edge of the pond. The man saw Ludwig and nodded approvingly as he listened to the music. Then he went on looking through the shallow ice of the pond in hopes of finding a turtle. At last he saw one and shouted. "Ah, there's a fine one!" He plunged a pointed stick through the ice and as Ludwig jumped to his feet, the man pulled out his knife and reached down into the icy water.

Ludwig raced toward him. In the seconds that it took him to reach the spot the young man had the turtle lying helpless on its back on the shore of the pond. He beheaded it with one quick stroke of his knife and, straightening up, grinned over at Ludwig. "Your music brought me luck, lad," he said. "I have spent the whole morning searching this pond, and, slap me, there's not another turtle in the whole of creation. At least not in this Godforsaken corner of it or my name is not Jonathan Woodstock."

Ludwig hardly heard a word Mr. Woodstock was saying. He stared at the turtle, which was big enough to make a splendid soup. Enough for General and Mrs. Washington and all the officers who were coming to the dinner. He looked and thought and as always when he was thinking his hands fingered his flute. "That is a mighty fine flute for such a young lad to own," Mr. Woodstock said and reached out toward it. "Mind if I try it?"

"Yes. No. I must catch another turtle!"

"Not a chance, my lad. Not the least bit of use even looking. I told you I searched every inch of the pond and there isn't another." With that Mr. Woodstock began to play the flute, but for once Ludwig couldn't even hear music. He could only lick his lips hungrily and stare down at the turtle.

"Sir," Ludwig began when Mr. Woodstock stopped playing. "Sir—I want—I need——I'd give anything I own for another turtle."

"I certainly don't doubt you'd like one," Mr.

Woodstock said and flipped the flute around his hand like a conjurer. "There is not a man Jack of us in the whole of Valley Forge who would not enjoy a good bowl of soup."

"No! No! I would n-not t-taste it myself," Ludwig stammered. He couldn't think straight without the flute in his hands. So now his words sounded forced and queer and as though he were lying, even in his own ears. "I w-want the t-t-turtle for General Wa-Washington."

Mr. Woodstock shrugged and held the flute out of Ludwig's reach. "Enough to pay for it with your flute?"

"No. No. I can't! It-it-isn't really mine." Cold fear made Ludwig's words clumsier and more stammered than ever. He jumped up and down like a foolish puppy, trying to reach the flute Mr. Woodstock held above his head.

"So the flute is not yours?" Mr. Woodstock said. "I might have known it was stolen."

"But it-it-isn't!" Ludwig got out. "Grandfather gave it to me to play in the band. He d-did not know they w-would set me to work as cook's h-helper!" Still stammering and sputtering and trying not to cry, Ludwig told Mr. Woodstock all about Grandfather von Zarn and Master Bridgeman and everything that had happened that morning.

When he stopped for breath Mr. Woodstock

31

moved a few steps away from him. "Very well," he said and put the flute in his own pocket. "I shall let you prove your story. You may take the turtle and after I know that the general has supped on it I shall return your flute. Meanwhile a friend of mine will know if it really came from Bavaria."

"It did. I swear it did. Grandfather played for the King's Hussars."

"Splendid. Excellent." Mr. Woodstock turned and walked away with swift, long-legged steps. "And soon, if your story is true, you shall have it back again. But in the meantime, my lad, don't forget the turtle." Ludwig wanted to shout and run after Mr. Woodstock, but the man was already out of sight and Ludwig knew he could never catch up with him. He looked down at the turtle and now he felt as hopeless as the creature in front of him. Would Mr. Woodstock ever return his flute? Or had he, Ludwig, simply been tricked out of it for nothing more than an ordinary turtle? He realized now that he didn't know Mr. Woodstock's company or regiment or even where in the whole of Valley Forge camp he was quartered.

I was a fool, Ludwig thought, and as he remembered how he had promised his grandfather to take care of the flute he felt worse than ever. He stood still for a moment, and finally, feeling as though he were moving in a nightmare, he walked the long way back to the headquarters kitchen.

Master Bridgeman was facing the spit by the open fire when Ludwig got back, but Private Scopes saw him come in. "Here's that lazy lad," he said, and instantly Master Bridgeman wheeled from the fire and started unbuckling his wide leather belt.

"Now you shall——!" he began, but when he saw the turtle Ludwig was carrying his expression changed. "Bless my stars. A turtle. And a fine fat monster to boot."

Ludwig wanted to explain what the turtle had cost him and ask if anyone in the kitchen knew of an artillery man named Woodstock, but Master Bridgeman waved him silent. "Not a word, boy. No need to say how you came by the creature. It is here in time for the general's dinner and that is what matters. Now you, Lanky, and you there, Scopes, sharpen the knives and we shall have the turtle out of his shell and into the soup pot in a twinkling."

For the rest of the day the hopeless feeling of living a nightmare stayed with Ludwig. He raked ashes and carried wood and turned the spit as Master Bridgeman told him. But all the while he couldn't feel or think of anything except his lost flute. At three in the afternoon when the dinner was served he saw Lanky and Scopes carry in the soup tureen without even wanting to peer around the door to see how the general and his lady might like it. He watched Master Bridgeman serve up the roast, but although he had hardly eaten all day he didn't even notice the fragrant smell. He just went on feeling numb as though losing his flute had taken the heart right out of him.

Time, which seemed gray and endless to Ludwig, passed. In the dining room healths were drunk and even the kitchen hands had a tot to celebrate General Washington's birthday. At the same moment there was the sound of band music outside. There was the snare drum, pipes, and tabors, the sound of an oboe, and above it all the clear thrilling tone of a flute.

Ludwig moved forward and now he didn't just peer around the doorway but almost fell over Private Lanky in his anxiousness to see. Was it possible, was it really possible that Mr. Woodstock belonged to the Fourth Artillery band and that he was going to return the flute the way he had promised?

General and Mrs. Washington and the officers smiled and applauded the music. Then General Washington spoke to one of his aides and a moment later the bandmaster and four flute players were brought into the dining room. "They say the general's very fond of flute music," Lanky whispered, but Ludwig didn't hear him. "He plays it himself back at home in Virginia."

Ludwig saw Mr. Woodstock and headed straight

toward him right in front of General Washington
and all the other guests. Privates Lanky and Scopes
tried to stop him, but Ludwig jerked himself free and
reached Mr. Woodstock. "My flute!" he said. "My
grandfather's flute. The general has supped, so remember your promise."

"Sh. Later!" Mr. Woodstock began, but General
Washington had seen and heard what had happened
and asked the bandmaster for an explanation. The
bandmaster turned to Mr. Woodstock, who saluted
smartly and told the whole story.

"It is the boy's flute, sir, and came to him from his
grandfather, who brought it from Bavaria," Mr.
Woodstock said. "Though I was not sure it was
Bavarian myself until I showed it to the bandmaster.
Ludwig, here, seemed too ragged and hungry to own
such a fine instrument. And when he said he wanted
a turtle I had just caught, not for himself, but for
Your Excellency's table it seemed wise to bargain
with him until I could be sure the turtle actually
reached the headquarters kitchen."

"Indeed it did and made a capital soup," General
Washington said and the other officers agreed. "A
capital soup indeed, so give the lad his flute. I should
like to hear him play."

As Ludwig's fingers closed around the flute he was
unaware of anything else. Then he felt the warmth
of the fire, and saw the bright reflection in the officers'

buttons and suddenly it came over him where he was. He started to scuttle back to his proper place in the kitchen, but Mrs. Washington stopped him. "The general has asked you to play, Ludwig," she said gently. "Any tune you like for His Excellency's birthday."

For an instant Ludwig was dazed with surprise. This was like his dream, only better, a thousand times better. But what should he play? His fingers moved over the stops of his flute and at that moment he knew! He began with "Who Is the Man?" and as the music spiraled upward from his flute, the words of it which he remembered—"Do good and evil quite eschew, seek peace and after it pursue"—seemed to him just meant to describe General Washington.

"Bravo." "Encore." "Give us another tune, lad," the officers said. Ludwig bowed and now he knew exactly what to play next. He put the flute to his lips and played "Yankee Doodle." This was the new, gay little tune which the redcoats had first played to make fun of the Colonials in Boston and the good Bostonians had taken it up and made it their own until it swept the Colonies.

This time when Ludwig put down his flute the rough, newly finished hut fairly cracked with the sound of applause. At last when Baron Steuben could make himself heard he spoke in his strange guttural voice. "Zounds, General Vashington! In thees country vy do you keep such a musician cleaning ze pots?"

There was laughter and more applause and as it died down, General Washington spoke to one of his aides. "See that the boy is transferred to the Fourth Artillery band," he said, and as he looked from Master Bridgeman to the bandmaster he added, "This order is to take effect at once." He turned back to Ludwig and now the lines in his lean, weather-beaten face were decidedly friendly. "Play that tune again, lad," he said, "It is a good air with which to end the evening."

So Ludwig played "Yankee Doodle" again and as the other flutes joined in, it sounded gayer, prouder, and livelier than ever. Ludwig von Bram was a member of the Fourth Artillery band!

SAINT PATRICK
AND THE LAST SNAKE

It was a warm balmy day and Saint Patrick was tired. He sat down under the shade of an old gnarled apple tree. Ridding all Ireland of snakes was not as easy as some people supposed and Saint Patrick needed a rest.

Some of the snakes he had driven into the sea, some he had driven into the rocks, and some he had magicked away entirely. It was easy enough when they wanted to be driven into the sea or wanted to be driven into the rocks. But sometimes they didn't. Then Saint Patrick had to fuss and fume until they did as he said, and that was what had made him hot and tired.

He sat down under the gnarled apple tree, and pretty soon he lay back in the soft grass that is so green it makes people call Ireland the Emerald Isle.

The grass was cool and restful and for a few moments Saint Patrick was at peace. For a few moments, but not for long. Soon a small black spider came out from the grass and crawled up Saint Patrick's neck and tickled him.

Saint Patrick slapped off the spider and settled back to his rest. He shut his eyes and thought how peaceful Ireland would be without the serpents. Just then there was a buzzing in Saint Patrick's ear. It wasn't a loud buzzing, but neither was it a peaceful buzzing, and Saint Patrick sat up again and slapped. It was a mosquito and Saint Patrick did not like mosquitoes one little bit.

When he had rid himself of the mosquito Saint Patrick lay down again, but he had hardly stretched out comfortably before he felt another crawly thing climbing up the side of his face. This time it was a shiny black bug that nipped at Saint Patrick's cheek when he screwed his neck around to look at it. Saint Patrick flipped the bug away with his thumb and forefinger.

"Begone!" he said. "And have done with you. Cannot a man have his rest?"

But it seemed a man couldn't, for soon there was the same black bity bug, or another one like it, climbing up the back of Saint Patrick's head. This time Saint Patrick sat up very straight and he was as mad as a saint can well be.

"Will you begone?" he said, "or shall I never be rid of ye? Surely if I free Ireland of serpents, there should be someone to rid me, once and for all, of these bothersome and biting creatures."

And with that Saint Patrick settled back for the third and last time. This time he really went to sleep and not one creepy thing bothered him.

He slept and he slept and at last when he woke up he felt refreshed. Saint Patrick was rested, and cool, and ready to go about his business. He sat up and stretched, and stood up and stretched, and he was just starting out on his way when he looked down and saw something that stopped him. There at his feet was the smallest, brownest snake in all Ireland.

The small brown snake said nothing, nor did it look the saint in the face. Instead, it wriggled quickly forward. Saint Patrick looked to see where it was wriggling and there right in front of the snake on the open part of Saint Patrick's sandal was another small black spider. The saint stared and the snake wriggled. The next instant the snake's small sharp tongue darted out and the spider was gone! It was gone without a shadow of a doubt, for the snake had eaten it.

As the snake glided off to a small sunny patch in the grass, Saint Patrick stood and looked at it.

"Well," he said, and his voice still sounded peaceful and rested and friendly. "So that's how it is? I rid

Ireland of the serpents and you rid Patrick of biting things."

He stood and frowned thoughtfully, looking down at the snake. It was a very small snake and it never looked at Saint Patrick with its bright unwinking eyes. Instead, it just lay sunning itself. Whenever a bug or a fly, or any kind of a creepy-crawly creature passed nearby, out shot the snake's sharp little tongue and the creepy, crawly creature was no more.

"I could drive you into the sea," said Saint Patrick. "Or drive you into the rock, or magic you away entirely." Still the snake said nothing, but lay coiled in the warm sunshine. "Or since you got me my rest," the saint went on, "I could get you yours."

The snake paid no attention to what Saint Patrick was saying. It simply lay coiled in the sun until a mosquito buzzed close to its head when the little snake's tongue darted out and there was no more buzzing.

"That settles the matter," said Saint Patrick and he pointed at the snake just as though he were going to magic it away entirely.

But the small, brown snake didn't magic away. It lay quite still and as it lay it grew harder and harder to see. It was no longer brown; no, nor nearly brown; nor yellowish brown. It was a bright emerald green, just the color of the grass of Ireland.

"There," said Saint Patrick, when he could hardly

see the snake himself. "There, and now you are safe, you and all your kind. Other birds and beasts cannot see you. And as for man, surely no one would harm a little snake that is as green as Ireland herself and spends its days adding to the peace of mankind."

CHINATOWN
APRIL FOOL

It was April Fool's Day and the fourth grade was going on a trip to Chinatown. As they started off, Sammy Hunt saw the old green purse on the sidewalk and grinned to himself. Sammy knew all about that purse and the thin piece of string that was tied to it. In fact Sammy had fooled Jamsie O'Reilley with that same purse as they had walked to school earlier in the morning. But Maisie Oakes didn't know anything about that. "Oh, look!" she said. She reached out and tried to pick up the purse just as Jamsie jerked on the string and pulled it out of the way.

"April fool!" Jamsie said and he laughed like anything. "The purse is empty."

For a second Maisie just stared and then she

laughed too and held out her little red pocketbook. "April fool, yourself," she said. "My daddy gave me two whole quarters to spend in Chinatown, so I don't mind one bit."

All the children laughed and joked as they followed Miss Harris to Chinatown. Sammy started to laugh but as he slipped his hand into his right-hand pocket, his laugh froze. Where there had been three dimes and a nickel just a little while ago there was nothing but a hole. There was just a mean ragged rip at the bottom of Sammy's pocket and no money at all. Sammy tried his left-hand pocket and now he felt more like crying than laughing. His watch was there and the shoestring watch fob which he had made for it, but nothing else. All the money he had saved up to spend in Chinatown was gone. It had slipped out of the hole in Sammy's right-hand pocket without his knowing it. And that wasn't any April-fool joke either. It was true and there wasn't a single thing that Sammy could do to change it.

By the end of the next hour Sammy knew he didn't like Chinatown one little bit. How could he when he had to stand around looking at the gay shopwindows while all the other children went inside to spend their money? There were china spoons, back scratchers with long ivory fingers, puzzles, boxes, and all sorts of fascinating little gadgets in the shopwindows. There were also baseball bats, elephants, cats, and dogs and fishes as small as the end of Sam's little finger. Any one of them would be perfect to put on the end of his watch fob if only he had the money to buy one. But he didn't have a dime or a nickel or even a penny. All his money had gone through the rip in his pocket.

"Now we're going down to the Chinese theater," Miss Harris said when the other children had finished their shopping, "and then we'll have to start home."

The sooner the better, Sam decided. Chinatown was a dud. Even the Chinese people walking along the street were a disappointment, dressed in dark city clothes like everyone else. A few of the houses had brightly painted gables, but most of them were quite dull, and the theater would probably be dull, too. Only the shops were exciting, and Sammy couldn't shop without money.

Miss Harris crossed a narrow alley and led the class down the hill toward Grant Avenue. Suddenly Sammy had an idea. He could take a short cut down the alley and around the block and meet the class at the theater. He'd get there as soon as they would, and he wouldn't have to look in the windows or hear the others talk about what they'd bought. He'd be there first and call out "April fool!"

Sammy looked around him and then ducked down the alley. Nobody missed him, and nobody called after him.

The alley was narrow and quite deserted, and there were no bright shopwindows. Colored clothes flapped on a line overhead, and on the wooden doorways he could see faded paper signs printed in Chinese.

Suddenly Sammy was aware of the stamping of his own shoes. He stood still and listened. Not a window opened, not a door shut. The distant whine of cable cars on Telegraph Hill was the only sound.

Sammy moved around a bend in the alley. Now even the hum of traffic was cut off. His heels sounded like pistol shots. Sam walked on tiptoe. Then, suddenly, he heard the sound of soft, padding footsteps behind him. He looked back, and for a moment his heart stood still.

There was a man following him, a Chinese in robe and queue. In his hand was a naked, glittering knife!

For one second, Sammy hesitated. Then he began to run. He had no choice. He had to go farther into the alley. If he turned back, he would run straight into the man with the knife. Sam ran, and his heart beat up in his throat. Once he looked over his shoulder. The Chinese was still close behind him.

Sam spurted, and then stopped dead. Another Chinese had glided silently out of the doorway in front of him! He was also dressed in silk, and he also carried a knife. Sammy shrank back.

In that second the first man caught up with him— and passed him!

The two Chinese nodded and hurried along together. Sammy gasped with relief. They weren't after him! They hadn't even noticed him. They were busily hurrying somewhere together.

Sammy walked along, and soon he was nearly at the end of the alley. He could see the cars in the street beyond. Between himself and the street was a low iron balcony. And under the balcony was a whole crowd of Chinese people in costume!

Sammy looked at their gay clothes and looked at the balcony, and then he understood. That bird cage of a balcony was the fire escape. And it was the fire escape on the back of the theater. These people were the actors. He had been scared shaky by two actors in fancy dress!

Sammy looked at the two men with the long knives, and then he laughed and laughed and laughed until he ached. The actor who had come up behind Sammy turned and looked at him curiously. "You all time laugh like sin," he said. "What is so funny?"

"It was an April fool on me," Sammy said when he could stop laughing. "I was scared goofy!"

"April Fool? Goofy?" The Chinese actor sounded puzzled, so Sammy told him all about April Fool's Day. He also told him all about how really-truly-no-fooling scared he himself had been just a few moments ago.

"Ah, now I understand!" the man said. "I am Lin-

53

Po, the actor, and you have just complimented the ferocity of my disguise." With that he moved toward Sammy, brandishing his knife. Sammy jumped out of reach. Then he looked up at Lin-Po and thcy both laughed. Sammy had been fooled all over again.

Lin-Po turned and spoke to some of the other actors. He spoke in a guttural rumbling Chinese that never changed its tone. Sammy listened, and then saw the others moving toward him. Apparently Lin-Po had told them the joke and all about April fool.

When he was finished he turned back to Sammy.

"Always, before the play," Lin-Po explained, "we meet outside."

Sammy looked up at the theater. He could understand that. There didn't seem to be enough room for the audience, let alone dressing rooms for the actors.

The actors made a circle around Sammy. There were three men, two women, a little boy of seven, and a girl of about five. The boy wore a red silk robe that came down to his silk slippers, and he had a broad sash around his waist. In his arms he had a small white cat.

Lin-Po beckoned to the little girl, and she came up and made a deep bow to Sammy. Sammy looked around, and then he made a bow back. There didn't seem to be anything else to do. He felt a little foolish, but, then, none of his class was there to see him. Be-

sides, you couldn't treat a girl who had on trailing, green silk the same as a girl in a play suit.

"She is called Almond Blossom," Lin-Po said. Sammy bowed again. Lin-Po looked pleased, and so did the little girl.

Lin-Po motioned to the Chinese boy to come forward. The boy handed his cat to his sister before he made his bow. When he was through, he reached for it again. But his eyes were still staring at Sammy, and so he missed the cat. She dropped on all four feet on the sidewalk!

The cat stood still for a fraction of a second. Then, as the little girl reached down, she sprang away. The cat shot across the alley so fast that she looked like a flying ball of white fur. She jumped up on the theater wall and onto the balcony. From there she looked down blinking at everybody below her.

"Kitty-White, come back," the little girl called.

The boy called in Chinese, and Lin-Po called in both Chinese and English. Then he turned to the children and spoke a stream of growling, biting Chinese words.

It was as plain to Sammy as if they had spoken English. They needed the cat for the play. The children had been careless. The play was due to begin in a few minutes. The cat was lost!

Lin-Po reached up toward the balcony, but even the ladder hanging from it was three feet out of his reach. The other actors crowded around, talking in Chinese and in English. They tried, but none of them could reach the balcony. The little cat's ears were cocked forward, its head was on one side. It was laughing at them!

Sammy hurried forward directly under the balcony. He couldn't possibly jump, but if he could climb, he might be able to reach the cat. He pointed to the ladder. "If you'll lift me up that far, I could climb," he told Lin-Po.

Lin-Po lifted him up on his shoulder without a word.

Sammy reached for the ladder and then hung there kicking. He chinned himself up on the lowest rung and began to climb. He could see the two Chinese children in their silk robes. Neither of them could have climbed after the cat in those clothes.

But it wasn't as simple as Sammy expected. Whenever Sammy put out his hand, the little white cat moved away. She bent her soft legs and sprang from a standstill up the wall of the building. Sammy looked after her and felt very foolish.

Then he looked down at the bright crowd of laughing actors. He couldn't be scared again. He had been frightened of Lin-Po and his knife, and that was enough. Sammy found a toe hold in the crumbling brick wall of the theater, and began to climb. He put one foot on top of a big wooden sign that was written in Chinese. He tested it, and it held his weight. He swung up carefully.

The cat was on a little ledge just above him. She looked down at him and as Sammy looked back into her yellow-green eyes she blinked and yawned just as though she were fooling him on purpose. Sammy flattened himself against the side of the building. He dug one hand into the bricks, until his finger tips hurt. One-two-three! "Here Pussy, here!" He let go with his left hand and swung for the cat. He caught her by her soft neck.

In another moment he scrambled back to the balcony, the cat under his arm. He climbed down the ladder. "Good! Well done, oh, excellently done," Lin-Po called up to him.

The other actors thanked Sammy in English and Chinese as they went into the theater. "It is time," someone said. "We begin."

The little girl looked up at Sammy, her eyes large and admiring. Sammy handed her the cat, and the next moment an older woman whisked her into the theater.

Only Lin-Po was left behind. "Well done," he said. "We are most grateful." He twisted something at his wrist and put it into Sammy's hand. "For you," he said, "with thanks."

In another moment he was gone, and Sammy was alone in the quiet alley. Sammy looked in his hand

and then looked again. There in his palm was a small, wooden cat. It was as sleek as silk and as cool to the touch as crystal. Sammy turned it over. It was an ornamental button, the threads still hanging from it where Lin-Po had torn it from his sleeve. Sammy looked at it and rubbed it with his fingers. It would make a watch fob, a beautiful watch fob, that would remind him always of Chinatown.

He walked out of the alley and met his class just going into the theater.

"Why, Sammy, I thought you were lost," Miss Harris said. "What shop were you in?" She ushered Sammy into the theater with the other children before he could speak.

"What'd you buy?" Tip Harrower asked and pulled out his lucky glass elephant.

Sammy looked at it and said nothing. Those glass toys were meant for tourists. He pulled out his cat and held it out in his hand.

"Gee," said Tip, "look at the Chinese cat. Where'd you ever get that?"

Just then the curtain went up, and Sammy sat down. He could see the two children and the cat, and Lin-Po holding the long curved knife which had scared Sammy so when he had first seen it.

"A friend of mine gave me the cat," Sammy said, and nodded toward the stage. "A Chinese actor friend. And that's no April fool joke either."

PINNEY'S EASTER HUNT

It was Easter Sunday, but there was nothing very Eastery about the farm. The wind was cold and raw, the tan fields were still hard with frost, and only the maples in the south pasture were bright with red bud.

Pinney shivered as he pulled on his old wool jacket and went out to do the chores. You felt colder when you knew it was meant to be spring and still the world didn't warm up. It was knowing how good things could be that made them seem so very bad when they didn't turn out the way you'd hoped they would. Like Pinney's knowing he had been asked to the Easter Hunt over in Wainbridge this afternoon when he couldn't leave the farm.

Pinney hurried up to the barn and tried not to think about the Easter Hunt, but that was impossible. You just couldn't help thinking about an egg hunt where they were going to give two live Bantam chickens to the boy or girl who found the most eggs. Pinney waved to Grandpa and tried to chase away his thoughts. It wasn't Grandpa's fault that he had to milk all the cows and couldn't spare the time to drive Pinney all the way over to Wainbridge. And it wasn't Granny's fault that she was just getting over the grippe and couldn't drive Pinney over, either.

Pinney fed the chickens and the pigs. It certainly wasn't his grandparents' fault, but that didn't help. If only he hadn't known that there was even a chance of his winning a pair of Bantams he would have been better off.

Pinney picked up a trowel and a basket in the woodshed and went into the woods. The twigs still snapped frostily underfoot as they had in December, but at least now there were birds chirping, and as Pinney neared the swamp he saw green pincushions of skunk cabbage, which showed that it wasn't mid-winter.

After a little while Pinney dug his hands in his pockets and began to whistle. He hoped he would find the hepatica soon. He was cold and what he really wanted to do was to go home and read in front of the fireplace. But he wanted to please Granny, too, even if the March wind that cut in under his collar seemed colder and meaner than any wind all winter.

Pinney kept on and on. He passed over Grandpa's

boundary and walked onto Mr. Leggett's farm. Mr. Leggett was one of Pinney's friends and never minded his trespassing, but reaching his farm made Pinney realize how far he had gone from home. If he hadn't found any hepatica so far, there wouldn't be another chance until he reached a sheltered place below a ledge of rock in the middle of the Leggett's wood lot.

When he finally reached the ledge Pinney's marching whistle suddenly quickened. Hepatica! Lots of it. Pale, pale lavender flowers with a deep green leaf. Piney looked around at the protecting arms of the rock ledge approvingly. Nothing but the warm south wind could blow in here. It was a perfect natural shelter.

Pinney picked out three good plants, dug them carefully, and placed them in his basket. They had good long roots so Granny could transplant them later into her flower garden. He was just covering the roots when he heard the little noise behind him.

Ba, ba, ba. It was such a feeble little noise Pinney wasn't even sure he'd heard it. Ba, ba, the sound repeated, and Pinney twisted around on his heels. For a second he didn't see anything and then, as its little black nose wriggled, he saw the lamb!

It was small and woolly, and Pinney knew it must be very newly born! He patted its small round head and wondered why its mother had left it. Grandpa didn't raise sheep and so Pinney knew it was one of

Mr. Leggett's flock. Perhaps Mr. Leggett or Jake MacTavish, his shepherd, had overlooked it. Except for its nose and its black-stockinged legs, the lamb was a perfect match with the gray rock behind it. Even if the lamb had been overlooked, Pinney was sure someone would be back soon to carry it home.

He petted it for a moment and held it in his arms. It nestled close to him and trembled as if it needed his warmth. But Pinney put it down again. It stood uncertainly on its wobbly legs looking very forlorn. He mustn't get fond of it. It would probably be safe here, and surely Jake would come after it soon.

Pinney started picking up his trowel and basket, but he didn't feel like leaving. He wished Mr. Leggett or Jake would come back while he was there. He'd feel better if he saw them starting off with the lamb in their arms. Right now it looked awfully lonely and pathetic, even in the shelter of the deep ledge.

Just before Pinney started off he turned to have one more look at the lamb. It was much too weak to try to follow him. It lifted its little head, but even that took too much strength and soon its head dropped back against its woolly chest. Pinney tried to leave. But then all of a sudden, he knew he couldn't go away without the lamb.

He couldn't take a chance on Jake or Mr. Leggett not finding that lamb. He'd have to carry it home to them tonight. Even if the Leggett barn was still a long, long walk away, Pinney knew he would have to get there. He just couldn't leave the lamb by itself.

Pinney picked the lamb up in both arms, tucked it under his coat, and somehow gripped the basket in his finger tips. It was an awkward load, but Pinney was sure he could manage. He started his marching whistle again, only louder and quicker this time so that he would walk faster. He had a long way to go, and it was getting late. Left foot, right foot, left, right! Pinney went as fast as he could along the edge of the ledge, out of the protection of the woods, and across the wind-swept fields, up the long hill to the farmyard.

More than once he had to stop to repack his load. Either the lamb would move in his arms or the basket would slip in his stiff fingers. Then he would readjust his burdens, straighten his shoulders, and march on. It might have been safe to leave the lamb in the home field where Jake or Mr. Leggett would be sure to find it. It seemed safe. It probably was safe, but Pinney wasn't taking any chances. The little animal, nestling in his arms, was so small, so helpless. He spoke to it in a low voice and thought that it seemed to tremble less while he was speaking.

Jake was milking when Pinney finally reached the barn. The place was warm and steamy with the breath of the feeding cows.

"Here's one of your lambs," Pinney said. "Found

it by the ledge. Guess maybe it was lost." Carefully he unbuttoned his coat and showed Jake the lamb.

Jake took it up in his big gnarled hands. "Must be a twin to the black lambie the big ewe bore this morning," he said. "I brought home the blackie and couldna understand why the mither fashed herself so at leaving the ledge."

Pinney nodded and gave the lamb a last loving little pat. "Good night," he said and headed for the door without daring to look back at the lamb in Jake's arms.

"Good night, lad," Jake said. "You'll like be hearing from Mr. Leggett."

Pinney never even wondered what Jake could mean. He had much more important things to think about. In the first place he had to run home to keep from being late. In the second place he wasn't sure if he would be able to find any pots for the hepatica plants he had found in Mr. Leggett's wood lot. Most important of all, Pinney knew he'd have to stop thinking about the lamb. Otherwise it'd be even worse than thinking about the Easter Hunt in Wainbridge. Now that he knew just how cute and appealing a little newborn lamb could be, he'd ache all over with wanting to own one if he didn't put his mind on something else.

By the time Pinney reached home Granny was downstairs and dressed for the first time since she had been sick. She had on her best blue silk dress which she only wore for parties, and Grandpa was getting ready for something pretty special too. He was in the kitchen making flapjacks, which he only did for big days like Christmas and Easter or somebody's birthday.

Neither Granny nor Grandpa said anything about Pinney's being late. In fact Grandpa called out that supper wouldn't be ready for another ten minutes. So Pinney had time to look around in the cellar where he found two little red clay pots that were just right for the hepatica plants. He gave them to Granny just as they sat down for supper. She hugged him and thanked him as though he'd given her three dozen store-bought roses all for herself. "This really is an Easter party," she said and nodded toward Pinney's place at the table. There were two very specially hand-painted Easter eggs that Granny had decorated for Pinney herself. Then there was a chocolate rabbit that Grandpa had bought at the store and a whole plateful of Easter cookies.

"It's a super-duper Easter party," Pinney said. "Thanks a million." He poured some syrup over the flapjacks Grandpa had made and at the same time he promised himself he wouldn't ever think about the Wainbridge Easter Hunt and the two Bantams again.

It was an easier promise to make than to keep. The very next morning Pinney woke up wondering who had won the two Bantams. That left him with a queer flat feeling that pressed down all over him. He jumped up and raced into his clothes. He was not going to start the day thinking about those Bantams. He was simply not going to do it.

He had just begun his breakfast when Granny called to him. "Been up to the barn yet, sonny?" she asked and her voice sounded pleased and mysterious at the same time. "Been up to the barn yet to feed the pigs?"

When Pinney was all through his oatmeal and his fried eggs and bacon he went up to the barn. Grandpa was tinkering with the tractor in the shed but when he saw Pinney he dropped his tools. "Been over to the barn yet?" he asked and he too sounded mysterious.

Once Pinney was inside the barn he understood. There, right in front of him, was the little lamb he'd returned to the Leggetts yesterday!

The lamb's little black nose was the same. Its black-stockinged legs were the same. Its round tennis-ball head was the same. It just looked a little stronger, and around its neck on a piece of green raffia was hung an envelope. Pinney went nearer and saw his name on the outside.

He pulled it open and looked inside. "Happy Easter," he read. "And good luck. See if you can bring this lamb up as well as you brought him home."

"He's yours to keep," Grandpa said. "Tom Leggett brought him over this morning. Said any boy who had the gumption to take so much trouble to bring a lamb home ought to own one. He brought along a nursing bottle for you to feed it with."

For a long time Pinney couldn't say anything. He just hugged the lamb and thought how it made a better pet than even the finest Bantams.

The lamb tried to lick his hands, and then suddenly Pinney spoke. "Just think! Suppose I'd gone to Wainbridge and nobody had found the lamb?"

PARADE FOR MAJOR PETTITT

It was a Saturday morning in late May and for once Joey Blake didn't have anything to do. He had thought of going swimming, but his mother said it was still too cold and wouldn't let him. He had thought of trying out a boat he had made on Beaver Brook but that was ten miles away and his father was using the car. Finally Joey decided to go downtown to find out about next week's Memorial parade. He walked all the way to the center of Daleville, only to learn that there wasn't going to be any Memorial Day parade this year. When Joey heard that he felt like kicking something hard. Memorial Day and no parade? A holiday and nothing special happening. What could be flatter?

Joey dug his hands in his pockets and started to walk home again. He turned down Elm Street and

73

at the second house from the corner he saw an old man in a wheel chair sitting on the front porch. Joey waved at the old man and gave him a snappy salute, but the old gentleman on the porch didn't answer. Joey walked on, feeling crosser and flatter and more let down than ever. The old man in the wheel chair was Major Pettitt, who was the oldest army veteran in Daleville. Major Pettitt had been an officer in the U. S. Cavalry ages ago, before even Joey's mother or father were born. In fact Major Pettitt had been one of Teddy Roosevelt's Roughriders and had fought at the battle of San Juan Hill in the Spanish-American War. And for years after he had left the Army he had been the leader of the Daleville Community Band.

Right now none of that seemed very exciting to Joey.

Old Major Pettitt was so old, so terribly old, that sometimes he didn't seem like a person at all. He was more like a wrinkled monument that all the boys in Daleville had been taught to salute.

As he crossed the street Joey looked back and saw old Major Pettitt look after him. His old head stuck out from his swath of blankets for all the world like a turtle stretching out from its shell. Joey grinned in spite of himself and saluted once more. He felt suddenly kindly toward Major Pettitt. Daddy always said the old gentleman was a lot brighter than he let on. Daddy said Major Pettitt didn't miss much even when he pretended to be asleep. Well, he didn't miss any boy who passed without saluting, Joey was sure of that. If you ever went by without snapping to attention, the old man was suddenly awake and tapping angrily on the porch floor with his cane.

Joey wondered who had started the custom of saluting old Major Pettitt and then he remembered. It had begun three years ago when the major was honorary marshal of the Memorial Day parade. Joey thought for a moment about that parade and suddenly he had an idea.

It wasn't just a passing thought, it was a real skyrocket of an idea. Joey Blake would organize a parade himself! If the grownups were getting lazy, that needn't stop the boys. They could have a boys' parade, a real humdinger with banners and bugles and everything. They could march from the playground in the middle of town all the way to Major Pettitt's. The old man would be thrilled and so would his granddaughter who took care of him.

Joey began to run straight for the town playground. He was going to round up the gang right then and there. He wasn't going to take any chances on having Memorial Day a holiday with nothing happening. If they couldn't do anything else they'd have a parade for old Major Pettitt.

The first person Joey saw was Eddie Keyes, who

was three grades behind him at school. Eddie was very young to be in a parade, but Joey asked him anyway. "Be in a parade?" Eddie said. "On Memorial Day? You bet! I'd love it!"

Joey dashed on to where some of the older boys were standing near the ball field, Gus Peters and Hally Myers and all the rest of the junior-high crowd. They were all Boy Scouts and their uniforms and bugles were going to help a lot. Joey couldn't be a Boy Scout himself until after his next birthday, but he counted on Troop 11. Hally Myers was the first person he asked. "Say, Hally," Joey began breathlessly. "How about being in a parade? A real parade. In honor of old Major Pettitt on Memorial Day."

Hally shook his head. "Sorry, Joe," he said. "I can't. I'm going down to Mill City to the Sportsman's Show on Memorial Day. The whole troop's going."

Joey looked at Gus Peters, hoping against hope that Hally was mistaken. But he wasn't. "That's right." Gus said. "Mr. Sims is going to take the whole troop and we're sure enough going to have fun."

Joey turned away without waiting to hear any more. When you took out the Boy Scouts there wasn't much left for a parade except little kids and a lot of girls. For a moment Joey thought of giving up his wonderful idea, but not for long. If he couldn't get the scouts he'd get whoever he could. "Fred," he called out, as two small boys walked toward him. "Fred Eagin, d'you and Winty want to be in a parade?"

The Eagin twins were too young even to be Cub Scouts but they certainly did want to be in a parade. So did Ralphy Hewlett, who was only six, and all the other small children who swung on the playground swings and slid down the chutes. All the girls wanted to be in the parade too. Joey wasn't so sure about the girls but they were sure about coming. "I've got a banner," Kate Myers offered. "A real Squadron A banner."

"I've got Daddy's bass drum," Mary Parkes said. "If somebody else'll carry it I can play it."

That seemed to settle it. The girls were in the parade. Joey looked after the group of Boy Scouts longingly as they moved off to the swimming pool. There were only five of them but they walked in step without seeming to think about it. They would have been a credit to any parade. Joey looked back at Mary and Kate and there seemed to be more girls flocking around them every minute. Girls wouldn't make it exactly military, Joey thought, but, after all, this was not a soldiers' parade. It was just a sort of congratulations parade in honor of old Major Pettitt.

"Come on over to our back yard," Joey called. "That will be the best place to practice marching. We want to make this the best parade ever."

The crowd followed Joey, but then his trouble really began. None of them, with the exception of Mary Parkes and Kate Myers, who were Girl Scouts, had ever marched in their lives. "You drill this half," Joey told Mary after a half hour of hopeless work. "And I'll drill the rest. Maybe if we divide 'em up, they'll do better."

Mary Parkes nodded briskly. "I might as well," she said. "I'll be in the lead anyway. The big drum always is."

Joey only grunted and tried for the fifth time to teach Ralphy Hewlett the difference between his left and his right foot. The parade was not turning out the way he had planned but there wasn't anything he could do about it now. He hoped that anyway old Major Pettitt would be pleased.

The crowd practiced every day after that, and by the end of the week they really were much better. The Eagin twins were still given to tripping up each other. Every once in a while Eddie Keyes got the giggles so that he had to stop marching, but except for that, things were going pretty well.

Two days before Memorial Day, Joey went home after a long practice to find Mr. Sims, the Scout Master of Troop 11, talking to his father. Joey went over to shake hands. "Glad to see you, Joe," Mr. Sims said. "As a matter of fact I really came specially to see you. The troop wondered if you'd like to go down with us to the show? You'll be joining us so soon that everybody thought it'd be all right and we'd like to have you."

Joey didn't say anything for quite a while and then all he could say was, "Boy!"

Finally he turned and looked at Mr. Blake. "How about it, Daddy? May I go?"

Mr. Blake got up and walked toward the window. "It's all right with me," he said. "I was just wondering about old Major Pettitt's parade and all your marchers. Wouldn't it leave them rather in the lurch?"

It seemed to Joey that the sunlight faded right out of the living room and left it cold and gray. Mary Parkes was pretty good with the bass drum but none of the boys would obey her unless Joey made them. He had to be on hand or the parade would fall through. When Joey thought of that he knew he couldn't go to the Sportsman's Show.

"Well, how about it?" Mr. Sims asked. "I must say I thought you'd jump at the chance."

Joey didn't trust himself to stay in the room. He turned around and hurried toward the stairs. "I can't go," he said over his shoulder. "Thanks. Thanks a lot but I can't go."

The next day the parade practice was worse than ever. It would be still worse on Memorial Day, Joey decided gloomily. Probably much worse. The whole parade would be a dud and Major Pettitt would just tap his cane crossly on the porch floor and laugh at them. Joey swallowed hard because his throat was stiff and uncomfortable. "Ralphy Hewlett," he snapped, and for the first time in all those drills his voice sounded cross. "You've got to learn which is the right foot or get out of the parade."

Ralphy nodded and it looked exactly as though his throat hurt too. "I'm trying, Joey," he said. "Honest I'm trying but I keep getting mixed up."

When Memorial Day finally came it was a clear, sunny morning and Joey tried not to think how perfect it would be at the Sportsman's Show. Instead he spent his time shining his shoes and getting his clothes ready. Of course, as the parade marshal, he should have walked in the lead and carried a baton, only he didn't have one. He didn't own anything even like a baton but perhaps it didn't matter. Mary Parkes had said that she was going to be in the lead or they couldn't have her big bass drum. So Joey wasn't going to look much like the parade marshal anyway. It doesn't matter, Joey told himself, and rubbed fiercely at his shoes. Nothing matters except getting Memorial Day and the parade over and done with!

A few hours later when the parade had started Joey felt a little bit more cheerful. At least everybody was there on time and they had all done the best

they could about their clothes. Most of the girls had on their Girl Scout uniforms, a few of the very little boys had on sailor suits, and the others had on anything they could get which seemed right for a parade. Joey himself was dressed in his Cub Scout uniform, which was too small for him, and his father's Korean War helmet, which was too big for him.

When they were all in line Mary Parkes looked over her shoulder at Joey and Joey nodded. "Forward march!" she shouted and gave the drum a resounding wallop. Boom! Tzing. Boom! Tzing. Boom! Boom! Boom!

In no time at all they were in front of the Pettitt's house. Even from the corner the house had not looked quite familiar but it wasn't until they were right in front that Joey understood why. Instead of just Major Pettitt sitting alone, the porch was crowded with people. Mother and Father, Mr. and Mrs. Parkes, Mr. and Mrs. Eagin and Miss Eagin, Mr. and Mrs. Hewlett, and Ralphy's baby sister. Everyone in town seemed to be there, and right in the middle of them sat old Major Pettitt, only this time he wasn't in his wheel chair. He sat on a straight Windsor chair and he wasn't wrapped in blankets. For the first time since the parade three years ago he was dressed in his uniform.

"Company, present arms!" Mary Parkes shouted, and her voice sounded very high and shrill. Joey could have done it better himself, but then Mary had had the bass drum and if she wanted to shout the orders, he had to let her. "Salute," said Mary and everyone, even Ralphy Hewlett, saluted with the right hand. "Three cheers for Major Pettitt," said Joey, because they'd planned that too. "Hip, hip, hurrah!"

When they finished cheering everyone on the porch clapped and then suddenly there was a silence. Joey felt a little uncomfortable. He hadn't planned what they were going to do after the parade. He supposed they could all march back again to his house, but that seemed a little flat. Suddenly there was a ripple of motion on the porch and people began getting up to get out of someone's way. "It's Major Pettitt! He's coming down!" Ralph Hewlett whispered in a voice that you could have heard across Daleville. "He's going to talk to us."

Ralphy was right. Old Major Pettitt was coming down the stairs, holding on to the handrail with one hand and a heavy wooden cane with the other. When he reached the bottom of the steps he stood and stared at the children without speaking. " 'Tention!" he said at last and his voice sounded even older and rustier and crustier than he looked.

The children all stood up very straight and tall. Joey was so relieved they'd done what Major Pettitt told them that he forgot how big Dad's helmet was and it almost fell off. He managed to get it back on

84

his head as Major Pettitt began to walk slowly along the line of parade. It was a long walk for Major Pettitt but he didn't cut out any of it. He looked at every single child in the parade and Joey felt sure he wasn't missing anything. He knew that Major Pettitt would see if anyone's buttons had popped off, or if their shoes were dusty. "At ease!" Major Pettitt said finally and once more the children did as they were told.

Joey gave a big sigh of relief and this time his helmet did fall off. He caught it against his shoulder but as he put it on again he knew that old Major Pettitt had seen what had happened. "Fall out!" Major Pettitt said and nodded at Joey.

Joey stepped out of line. He was so embarrassed he felt as though he were bursting right out of his clothes. It wasn't his fault that he'd outgrown his Cub Scout uniform or that Dad's helmet was too big for him. It wasn't his fault at all, but now Major Pettitt was going to make a fool of him in front of everybody.

For what seemed to Joey like ages and ages Major Pettitt didn't say a word. He just looked at Joey as though he was trying to look right through him. "Joe Blake, I hear you are the general," Major Pettitt said at last and his voice sounded rustier and crustier than ever. "I hear you are the general who wouldn't leave his troops. Not even, why, not even to go to the Sportsman's Show in Mill City."

A hot embarrassed red crept further and further up Joey's throat and ears. What was this? What was old Major Pettitt saying? But the major was through speaking. He turned now and reached for a long slender package which his granddaughter had been holding and handed it to Joey. "For you, my boy," Major Pettitt said. "For you. For sticking with your troops."

Joey looked down at his package and even before he had the last paper off he knew what was inside. It was a drum major's baton! A beautiful silver wand topped with a brass ball. It was the very one that Major Pettitt had used in the days before he grew too old to lead the Daleville Community Band in the Memorial Day parade.

When Major Pettitt reached the porch he looked back before the two men helped him to his chair. "Congratulations," he called. "Congratulations."

Joey snapped back to attention and his baton flashed upward in a proud salute. In fact it knocked his helmet right off his head but nobody noticed it. The children and all the grownups and even old Major Pettitt were too busy cheering to notice anything. "Three cheers for Joey Blake," they shouted. "Three cheers for Joey!"

FUNG'S FOURTH

It was the Fourth of July and a perfectly beautiful day. From all over Central City children and grownups were going to Lakeside Park. There was to be a parade in the park in the daytime. Then, late at night in the dark, there was to be a special Fourth of July fireworks celebration by the park lake. Everybody in Central City wanted to see the parade and the celebration. So they hurried to Lakeside Park on buses and the subway, in cars and on bicycles, on foot and on roller skates.

Wang Fung walked from his home to the park. It was a long walk but Fung had started early, so he reached the park before noon. Fung turned down one of the park paths that led to a place where there were a lot of statues. Then he saw that David and Pierre and Marta and Jan and other children from all over Central City had reached the park ahead of him. When Fung saw the children he began to run as fast as his short fat legs would carry him.

Fung's family had only moved to Central City from a farm a few months ago. So Fung had never seen a Fourth of July parade and celebration. Of course Fung had heard stories about the Fourth of July ever since he could remember. He knew that the Fourth of July was America's Independence Day. He knew it was the day when all the people in Central City and in other towns and cities all over the country got together to show how proud and happy they were to live in America. There had never been anyone on the farm to get together with, so Fung was extra specially eager to see the parade and the celebration at Lakeside Park.

Right now the children who had reached the park ahead of Fung were shouting and waving to him.

"Hurry, Fung!" Jan Matchak called to him. "Hurry."

"Oh, goody. Fung's here," Martha Ludwig said. "We've been waiting and waiting."

"Hurry up! Fung!" Tim O'Grady called out louder than any of the others. "We're going to have a Fourth of July parade of our own before the grown-ups have theirs."

The children started to parade right then and there in between all the statues. They walked by twos so as not to crowd other people. They made such a fine long line of marching couples that every once in a while Tim O'Grady, who was at the head of the parade, had to stop to let everybody catch up. The first time Tim stopped they were right in front of a statue of Count Casimir Pulaski. "And who in the world was the count?" Tim asked and spelled out the letters of the name at the base of the statue. "Who was C-A-S-I-M-I-R   P-U-L-A-S-K-I?"

"Why he was a Pole like my father," Jan Matchak said proudly. "He came over here to help America get free. He was a general in the Revolutionary War."

Fung looked at Jan as they started to march on again. Fung liked to see people happy and Jan looked very happy indeed. Fung didn't blame him. It must be grand to pass a statue of one of your father's countrymen who was a general in the American Army. They marched on past the lake and up the hill until they came to a statue of the Marquis de Lafayette. This time nobody had to ask who he was, but Pierre told them anyhow.

Pierre stuttered and it took him quite a long time

to tell his story, but Fung waited for the very last word. It was rude to interrupt when people talked about their ancestors and for today anyway, Lafayette, who was French, was a sort of ancestor of Pierre's.

They came to the statue of Columbus, and John, Tony, and Rosa, whose parents had come from Italy, took turns telling about him. Finally they came to the big statue of Carl Schurz and little Marta Ludwig, whose family had just come from Germany, told the other children all about him. "Carl Schurz was German," Marta said, "who came to this country to be more free. He lived here and worked here and wrote books. Then he wasn't German any more but an American the way I am."

Little Fung liked Marta's speech so much that he thought about it all during the picnic lunch, which the children ate at the edge of the park lake. Fung thought of what Marta had said so hard that he didn't really taste his food. He just sat and ate without tasting anything. And all the time Fung wished that he could point to something or someone Chinese and say now it was American the way he was.

It didn't have to be a statue of a great Chinese-American. In fact, when the policemen marched past in the grown-up parade after lunch and Tim O'Grady pointed out that most of them were Irish-American the way he was, Fung envied Tim even more than he had envied Marta.

After the parade the children sang songs and played games. Even those seemed to belong more to the other children than to Fung. They played "Taffy was a Welshman," which pleased David because his father came from Wales. They played "London Bridge Is Falling Down." That pleased Bill and Audrey and several other children whose families had come from England either just recently or so long ago they had fought in the Revolutionary War. They even sang "*Ach, Du Lieber Augustin*" and Marta Ludwig taught them some of the German words.

By the time Fung had to go home to supper he felt a little tired and very, very lonely. It wasn't anybody's fault. No one had been mean to him or teased him. In fact all the children had gone out of their way to be nice and friendly. Right now they were calling out to him. "See you later, Fung."

"We'll see you after dark at the celebration."

"Be sure to get back in time so you won't miss anything!"

"Yes, hurry back. The celebration will be super! Even better than the parade."

As Fung walked home he wasn't at all sure that he wanted to come back to the celebration. It would be like the statues and the marching policemen and the games. It would be Scotch-American or Swedish-

American or French-American but never Chinese-American.

Fung ate his supper of rice without saying much. "You had better have a rest before you go to the celebration," Fung's mother said. "You look tired."

"Perhaps I won't go," Fung said. "I might just go to bed."

Fung's mother shook her head. "Oh, but that wouldn't be polite," she said. "Last week when I found I could not take you to the celebration Mrs. Kung Li was good enough to ask you to go with her. Mrs. Kung Li is old and lives alone and she is counting on you to keep her company. Besides, last week when she asked you to go with her you said you wanted to go very much indeed. It would be rude to change your mind now unless you are not well."

"I am well and I will go," Fung said. Then he went and lay down on his bed to rest before the celebration. He didn't feel sick at all, nor even tired any more but he still felt lonely and a bit cross. Mother was right as usual. He had told Mrs. Kung Li that he would like to go with her to the celebration. And he had meant it too. It was just that after the whole long day in which everything had been American this and American that without anything ever being Chinese-American he wasn't so sure he would like the celebration. Also he wasn't at all sure that Mrs.

Kung Li, who loved to talk about the long-ago days in China, would like it either.

It wasn't until Fung was finally back at Lakeside Park in the dark with Mrs. Kung Li that the cross and lonely feeling went away. In the first place the park looked bigger and stranger and much more exciting at night than it had in the daytime. The statues looked enormous and sort of scary when you couldn't see the heads very well in the darkness. Even the great black trunks of the trees looked grim and queer. Fung was sure that Mrs. Kung Li would have been very unhappy if she had had to walk past the statues and trees all by herself. Fung felt a bit scared himself and he was a boy and not a little old lady. So he stayed very close beside Mrs. Kung Li until they came to the edge of the lake where the celebration was to be.

Then Fung saw Pierre and Jan and Marta and lots of other children with their mothers and fathers or grown-up friends. Fung started to say "Hello" but before the word was out of his mouth the celebration started. It was a fireworks celebration put on by the city. Fung's "Hello" was just a round "O" of surprise and pleasure as he watched the first rocket swirling up into the sky.

There was another rocket and another. Then there was a giant salute that spangled the sky with a golden spray of fire. There were pin wheels and wonderful red, white, and blue balls of light that dropped down, down, down to earth on little white parachutes. There were more rockets and after that a fine polar bear made of little lights and a beautiful flashing waterfall. Finally at the very end there was an American Flag of red, white, and blue fireworks!

Mrs. Kung clapped her hands and Fung clapped his hands and all the other children and grownups clapped their hands.

"Oh boy, that was great," Jan said. "Much better than the parade."

"Sure was," said Tim. "Who'd you suppose ever thought of fireworks?"

Fung knew. He hadn't thought of it before but he did know. His little oval face broadened into a grin. "Why, the Chinese," he said. "My father's countrymen thought of it. They thought up fireworks many, many years ago."

"That is right," said Mrs. Kung Li as everyone jostled against everyone else on the way home. "Our Chinese ancestors used fireworks hundreds and hundreds of years ago."

"The Chinese were the first to make a compass too," Marta Ludwig's father said and looked at Fung over his glasses. "And they knew how to make printed books long before a German named Gutenberg started the first printing press in Europe."

"Sure and they are a very clever people," said

Policeman O'Grady, who was Tim's father. "And so kind and polite you'd be after thinking it was the Chinese invented good manners."

Fung didn't say another word. He was too happy to speak and almost too happy to listen. He just moved very close to Mrs. Kung Li because he was so pleased he'd come and grateful to her for taking him. She took his hand and gave it a quick little squeeze. "This was a perfect ending for a glorious day," Mrs. Kung Li said and suddenly Fung knew she was thinking just the same thing that he was. Fireworks were Chinese. The Fourth of July was American. So fireworks on the Fourth of July was a perfect Chinese-American celebration.

WESTWARD OVER THE
OCEAN SEA

One afternoon of late July in 1492 two boys hurried out of the monastery of La Rábida on the hill above Palos and went to the far end of the garden. Juan Rodríguez, the older of the two, looked over his shoulder to make sure they had not been followed. There was no one in sight! He gave a sigh of relief and pointed to a homemade pin wheel fluttering from a tree trunk just ahead of them. "There is my wind gauge, Diego. And, wonder of wonders, none of the friars has found it."

Little Diego Colón, the admiral's son, looked the pin wheel over carefully before he answered. "It turns well," he said finally. "But did you really make it all by yourself?"

"Of course, you silly goose! Do you think one of

the friars or his most strict lordship, the abbot, helped me?" Juan said, forgetting that since Diego had been made a page to the royal court of King Ferdinand and Queen Isabella he was not to be spoken to like any ordinary six-year-old. "I made it yesterday out of bits of my shirt when I should have been at choir rehearsal. The friars forced me to fast last night and this morning as a punishment, but at least none of them found out what I was making."

"Aren't you terribly hungry?" Diego asked. "And —and—afraid of what the friars will do to you if they do find out?"

Juan barely heard him, as he was too absorbed by the pin wheel to think of anything else. The breeze freshened and the little sails turned faster than ever! Juan took off his black, close-fitting cap and instantly the late afternoon sunlight turned his red, unruly hair into a fiery mop. At the same moment the monastery bells rang and little Diego clutched at his hand. "Juan, hurry!" he pleaded. "The vesper bells are ringing and we shall be late!"

"You go." Juan pulled his hand free as he spoke. "I'll be there in a minute." He leaned forward, his thin young body taut as a steel blade, and carefully fixed his cap to one arm of the pin wheel. For a moment the sails stopped turning and Juan held his breath for fear his own breathing would upset his calculations. Then, slowly at first but gaining speed,

the pin-wheel turned with Juan's cap at the end of one arm.

"Juan, please, please come!" Diego tried again before he scuttled off toward the monastery chapel. Juan never even knew when Diego left or the bells stopped ringing. He looked from his pin wheel down toward the harbor of Palos where Admiral Colón's three ships were riding at anchor, and beamed.

"The admiral is right and my wind gauge has proved it!" Juan was so excited he spoke aloud without knowing what he was doing. "The prevailing wind and the strongest blows to the westward. Yesterday afternoon at nones and this morning at matins my wind gauge turned to the west, and now at vespers when all winds slacken it still turns to the west carrying the weight of my cap."

Time passed and the sun began to set. Juan was unaware of anything except the bright dreams and brave fancies that stirred his heart like the sails of his pin wheel. As long as Juan could remember he had longed to go to sea, but no one had ever encouraged him about that. His parents were dead and the abbot said that as soon as Juan's voice changed he should be apprenticed to a weaver. Juan hated the idea of learning the weavers' trade and spending his life at a loom, but he seldom thought about it. Instead he filled his mind with every scrap of sea lore he could pick up. He pored over the two books of travel and geography in the monastery library whenever he was allowed to do so. He learned as much about the stars as Fray Antonio de Marchena, the astronomer monk, would condescend to teach him. Above all whenever there was an errand to be done in Palos, Juan asked to go, in the hope of getting a closer look at the ships in port and listening to the talk of the sailors.

It had all been fun but too chancy, too dependent on the whims and wishes of other people. But now with the wind gauge Juan had found something he could do on his own. Juan hugged himself because he was so happy and at that moment a man's stern voice rang out behind him. "Juan! Juan Rodríguez!"

Juan wheeled and saw Fray Antonio and Diego Colón coming toward him down the garden path. For an instant it shot through Juan's mind that Diego had told on him. The next second, as he saw Diego's worried face and pleading eyes, he knew the little boy hadn't been able to help it. Fray Antonio had simply seen Diego running toward the chapel and had realized where he had come from.

"Fray Antonio, it was not Juan's fault I was late for vespers," Diego said. "I asked him to take me out here to show me his pin wheel."

"You may go, Diego," Fray Antonio never took his eyes off Juan as he spoke. "Juan must pay the price of his own wickedness and folly. And you, Diego, are to report at once to the abbot."

As Diego went off he looked so small and miserable Juan felt sorry for him. Still, not even the abbot would punish a page to the Queen and so there was no need to worry about him. Juan looked back at Fray Antonio and for the first time realized his own difficulties. His wind gauge would be destroyed, of course, and after that what would they do to him? Beat him, hang him up by his thumbs, or make him go on fasting until his whole body ached from hunger? All three were possible, Juan knew, and shivered at the prospect. "I beg for pardon," he began, but Fray Antonio interrupted him.

"Pardon is not mine to give." The friar said and now his voice was not so much stern as dry and impersonal. "And the abbot does not take lightly your recent misconduct, especially not your leading young Diego into temptation. He feels that an orphan boy, like yourself, with nothing to recommend him except a treble voice, which will soon be changing, should be more careful. But now, Juan Rodríguez y Diva, look down at the harbor and tell me what do you see there?"

"Ships," Juan said, as much puzzled by the friar's use of his whole name as the strangeness of his order. "The Admiral Cristóbal Colón's three caravels, one of which is lateen-rigged, and a nao square-rigger.

And to the starboard two very small caravels, also lateen-rigged."

"Spoken like a sailor," Fray Antonio said and at his words hope rose like a rocket in Juan's heart. Was it possible? By the saints and our Blessed Lady, did Fray Antonio mean to persuade the abbot to let him go to sea? Juan started to speak but Fray Antonio waved for him to be silent. "What else do you see, my son? Up there toward Huelva and close to the quay?"

"Another caravel," Juan began, "this one is being loaded. With bales of cloth, I think, but it's hard to tell from this distance. The men are handling the bundles so carefully that the cargo must be something very precious."

"Precisely!" Fray Antonio's voice crackled like the parchment pages of an old book. "Precisely. The cargo is precious since it consists of bales of cloth from Master Martínez' looms. Because Master Martínez has found favor with our gracious Queen, who has deigned to use his material for the royal household, everything he does or owns is important, or, as you say, precious.

Juan reached out to the tree to steady himself. The sight of his pin wheel still turning with the wind gave him the courage to speak. "Is the money paid out?" he faltered. "I mean the fee which the lord abbot will pay to Master Martínez for my apprentice-ship?"

"No, not yet." Fray Antonio stared up at the sky as though by sheer will power he would see the stars while it was still daylight. "The fee has not been paid, but an agreement has been reached between our reverend father in God, the lord abbot, and the master weaver. That means, my son, that your future has been decided upon. No matter where you go, in the whole of Spain, the weaver has a right to six years of your labor."

No matter where you go IN SPAIN. The words repeated themselves over and over in Juan's mind. He reached out instinctively and took his cap from the pin wheel. The cloth sails fluttered and turned more quickly without the load, but Juan didn't notice. IN SPAIN the weaver had a claim to his time but only IN SPAIN. Surely Fray Antonio had told him all this to warn him to escape?

Juan looked up and saw that Fray Antonio was already walking away toward the chapel. The friar paused once and Juan thought he made the sign of the cross and murmured a farewell blessing. There was no way of telling for certain. When Fray Antonio reached the chapel steps he turned around and faced Juan. "The lord abbot instructs me to tell you that the first part of your punishment is to be meted out to you at midnight by two of the novices. These are strong young men, Juan Rodríguez, with strong arms from thrashing grain from the wheat stalk."

Juan hardly heard him. A beating, even until one's back bled, seemed as nothing compared to being bound out for six long years to a weaver. Just then the breeze freshened a trifle and instantly Juan's pin wheel whirled faster and more noisily. Juan turned toward it and as he listened to the rustle of the little sails, it seemed to him that the sound had words and a meaning. *The wind blows west to freedom. The wind blows west to freedom!*

Juan pulled on his cap and moved forward. Now was his chance to escape. Now, when everyone was either at chapel or in the refectory! He crept silently toward the empty dormitory, picked up his father's cross and his dagger, a handful of clothes, and slipped out again into the garden. He hesitated for a second as he passed the pin wheel. He wanted to take it with him but he knew he couldn't. The thing would be crushed to bits if he put it in his pack. If he held it upright the friars and the master weaver would find him by it without even trying.

He gave the sails a last loving turn and headed down the hill to Palos. He was breathless and half faint with hunger by the time he reached the port, but at least so far none of the friars or novices had caught up with him. By the time Juan reached the waterfront he dared move more slowly. It had grown much darker and surely if no one from the monastery had gone after him by now, they would wait until morning.

Juan came to a familiar tavern and stopped for breath by the door. He'd often lingered here when doing errands, hoping to hear tales of the mysterious islands which some sailors swore lay west of Gomera and others said did not exist at all. It was here that Juan had first heard of the piece of wood, clearly worked on by human hands, which some seafarer had found in the westernmost part of the ocean sea. And this story had given him the idea for his wind gauge.

Right now Juan was too tired and hungry and much too frightened to think about sea yarns or wind gauges. He waited until a noisy crowd of sailors pressed into the tavern and slipped in behind them. If he was lucky he might be able to pick up some crusts of bread and find a dark corner behind the kitchen where he could spend the night unnoticed. Then before daylight he must somehow sneak his way onto one of the ships in the harbor. Juan knew what happened to stowaways and the thought made him shudder. Still it was his only chance of escaping Master Martínez.

He stayed in the shadows and tried to judge his chances of picking up some food. At a table near him two men argued as to whether Queen Isabella had pawned her jewels to pay for Don Cristóbal

Colón's expedition or whether the citizens of Palos were putting up the money. The talk grew angry and one man slammed down his tankard, knocking a wedge of bread to the floor as he did so.

Juan moved forward, drawn like steel to a magnet, toward the piece of bread. It was a sin to steal, but surely there could be no harm in taking something that had fallen on the floor in front of him. He reached out and then a wonderful thing happened! From the other side of the room a tall man called out to him, "Here, boy. Leave that for the dogs and come and eat hearty."

Juan moved across the room and sat down where the tall man showed him. Meat, bread, cheese, and a fine bunch of grapes were set before him. It was more food than Juan was given at the monastery on a feast day and he ate it all. It was only when Juan had eaten the last mouthful that he realized that the tall man had pushed back his chair and was talking to the other men in the tavern. "Friends, come away!" the tall man said. "Come away with us on this voyage. . . . We shall find gold-roofed houses and you shall come back rich and happy."

It dawned on Juan that the man was recruiting, actually asking for, sailors and ship's boys to go on a voyage. He jumped to his feet but a sailor pulled him down again. "Be still young redhead," the sailor said. "And don't interrupt your betters. El Capitán Martín

Alonzo Pinzón is enlisting crews for Don Cristóbal Colón's great voyage. Every word is important."

Juan sat and listened with breathless attention. And now as Señor Martín Alonzo Pinzón spoke, his words stirred Juan's heart the way the west wind had turned his pin wheel. The voyage to find a short course to the Indies would be richly rewarded. More than that, Don Cristóbal, Admiral of the Ocean Seas, had a royal letter, fixed with the royal seal, which said that all persons sailing in his company were granted pardon for any wrongdoings they may have done before the day of departure. As Captain Pinzón finished, Juan sprang to his feet and this time the sailor did not hold him back. The man was up himself and hurrying over toward Pinzón's table.

By the time Juan stood in front of the tall sea captain he was speechless with excitement, but it didn't seem to matter. Captain Pinzón only grinned down at him and pointed to the list of the ship's company. "Tell me your name, young redhead," he said, "and I shall write it down for you on this roster and you can mark it with an X beside the letters."

"B-but I can wr-write, sir. And r-read, if it please you."

"Good lad, sign here then." Captain Pinzón gave Juan a clap on the back and shouted to his second-in-command to row Juan out to the ships with the others who had newly enlisted. "Take the young redhead to the *Marigalante*," he added. "There may be something under that flaming mop of his which could be useful there."

Juan did not understand everything that Captain Pinzón had said and he didn't care. All he knew was that he was actually going to sea. And to serve under the great Don Cristóbal Colón on his expedition to find a short route to the Indies! It was too good to take it all in so suddenly. Juan gave himself up to the joy of feeling the wind on his face, hearing the creak of the oarlocks and watching the riding lights of a caravel draw nearer. Juan was half asleep by the time they reached the ship and it wasn't until the next day that he learned he had been put on board the *Santa Maria*, which was the admiral's flagship.

"What is really her name?" Juan asked a young sailor when they finally had a breathing space between fetching and hauling and stowing away gear. "Last night Captain Pinzón called her the *Marigalante*."

The sailor grinned. "Only he would dare say that. Her name has been changed from the *Gay Mary* to *Saint Mary* after the blessed Virgin, by order of Don Cristóbal himself. When he comes aboard don't let him hear you call her anything else if you value your life. His hair is as red as your own and all *rojos* are quick tempered."

Juan bit his lip as it dawned on him that being on

the Admiral's flagship might be very risky. He was sure he had done little Diego no harm, but if Don Cristóbal had learned about it from the abbot he would have heard another story. The pardon which Captain Pinzón had spoken of cleared Juan as far as the master weaver was concerned, but if Don Cristóbal had listened to the abbot he might easily refuse to take him on the expedition. Still, things could be worse. Juan would simply have to stay out of the admiral's sight until they were safely at sea and trust to luck that he had not seen the abbot lately or even heard of the pin wheel.

The next few days of getting ready to sail and the weighing of anchor on August the third were not a bit like what Juan had expected. He was made to work for so long in the hold that he blinked like a mole when he came out in the daylight. The work was harder and heavier than anything Juan had ever done before and a crack of the boatswains cat-o'-nine-tails made the friars' beatings seem gentle.

Still Juan was at sea and that was what counted. Every day and especially at twilight when he joined the rest of the crew in singing the *Salve Regina,* he felt himself a sailor. As for the precious moments he could snatch on deck to watch the wind fill the *Santa Maria's* sails, they were so glorious that Juan felt he was living in a dream come true.

On the fourth day out from Palos, Juan had just

crept out on deck when a deep voice called to him. Juan jumped, thinking it was the boatswain. Then when he realized that none other than Don Cristóbal had spoken to him and asked his name and where he came from he was even more nervous.

"I am called Juan Rodríguez y Diva, Your Excellency," Juan said and remembered to take off his cap and bow the way he had been taught at the monastery. "I have lived in Palos since my father was killed fighting the Moors."

"Ah yes." Don Cristóbal's eyes seemed to go right through Juan to the tumbleline behind him. "And you can read and write, so the boatswain tells me. Where did you learn, lad?"

"At the monastery . . ." Juan began, and then when he realized what he was doing he stopped short.

"At the monastery of La Rábida where you sang in the choir," Don Cristóbal finished the sentence for him." Why did you leave so suddenly, boy? Your voice hasn't changed yet. I heard your treble last night when the crew sang the *Salve Regina*."

Juan's mouth felt dry again and his knees knocked together. Don Cristóbal must have heard the story of his pin wheel and Don Diego and had just realized that Juan was the culprit. Worse still, he had undoubtedly heard everything from the abbot himself. Juan sweated with fear and said nothing.

"You were to be apprenticed to a weaver," Don

Cristóbal went on. "The master weaver of Huelva."

"But—but the royal letter," Juan faltered. "Captain Pinzón said that it promised freedom and pardon."

"It is as he said." Don Cristóbal nodded, and Juan saw that the great man's hair was as red as his own. "And I take it you had no desire to be a weaver?"

"No, sir. No!"

"That I can understand," Don Cristóbal said dryly and Juan remembered a rumor that Don Cristóbal's father had worked with wool but that he had never wanted to follow that trade. Juan breathed more easily until Don Cristóbal began to talk about the kind of men and boys he wished to have serve under him. "Stouthearted souls and free," the admiral said. "Those with enough vision and faith to choose to go on this particular voyage. Are you certain, Juan Rodríguez, that escaping Master Martínez was not more on your mind than joining the crew of the *Santa Maria*?"

"No. Yes. No. Yes, sir. I would have gone on any ship to escape." As soon as Juan had spoken the truth he felt so limp and hopeless that he told Don Cristóbal every word of what Fray Antonio had said, and what he, Juan, had understood by it. As Juan finished, the wind freshened and he looked up and saw the billowing sails of the *Santa Maria*. "But I have always wanted to follow the sea," he murmured, and

it was almost as though he were talking to himself
and not to the thickset, stern-faced admiral whom he
was sure he had insulted. "I have dreamed of watching the wind and sailing with it to the westward.
That is why I built my pin wheel gauge in the monastery garden. To see for myself how strong and free
the wind blows toward the west."

At that moment the boatswain came in sight and
as Don Cristóbal called to him, Juan could guess
what would happen. A flogging, perhaps, and after
that chains until he was put ashore at the Grand
Canary. He could hardly expect less after everything
that had happened.

Don Cristóbal turned and put his hand for a moment on Juan's sore back. "This lad is to act as my
cabin boy," he said to the boatswain. "He is too
young and slight for his present tasks and it would be
a pity to break him. He has the makings of an excellent sailor."

"Aye, aye, sir! As the admiral wishes."

Don Cristóbal and the boatswain strode off and
for a moment Juan was left alone to stare upward at
the sails and the sky. The wind whistled in the rigging and now the meaning of the sound was as clear
or clearer than the words of the familiar chant which
Juan and the rest of the crew sang every evening.
You shall sail westward to adventure and freedom!
Westward with the Admiral of the Ocean Seas!

THE HALLOWEEN
BIRTHDAY

School is out. School is out! As the bell rang and clattered through the hall, the first and second grades spilled out into the October sunshine. School is out. School is out! Red sweaters, plaid skirts, and bright checked dresses made a whirly, twirly pattern across the schoolyard.

"Children. Children!" Miss Parker called from the schoolhouse steps, and for a moment the reds and greens and soft dungaree blues were still. "Don't forget tomorrow is Halloween. Be sure and wear your costumes to school."

"We will!" "We won't forget!" "See you tomorrow, Miss Parker."

The children moved on again toward the swings, toward the slides, toward the buses. A few who lived nearby began to walk and hop and skip toward home.

Across the playground the sun sparkled brightly on Danny's glasses as he turned to wave good-by. "I won't forget, Miss Parker." Then he started off again toward the little old back road that led down into the valley where he lived.

This morning Danny's mother had said for the first time he could walk home by himself. He didn't even have to wait for Tad and Mike, his twin big brothers in the eighth grade. So now Danny laughed out loud as he skipped along. There was no chance of his forgetting tomorrow. Tomorrow was Halloween AND Danny's birthday. It was his seventh birthday, and he knew it was going to be super-special!

There was going to be a supper party at Uncle Bill's and Aunt Bessie's house. Then there was the surprise combination birthday present that Uncle Bill and Aunt Bessie and Mother and Father were giving him.

Danny scuffed up an extra-big pile of clean, dry leaves and plopped down on top of them. The leaves were warm from the sun. They smelled good, and they felt good, and they sounded just wonderful.

Danny scooped up great rustling armfuls and made himself a fallen-leaf fort from which he could look down into the valley.

He saw his family's house and right across the cornfield he saw Uncle Bill's and Aunt Bessie's house and the cluster of farm buildings. The corn shocks looked like Indian tepees. For a second Danny thought maybe his surprise combination present was going to be a tent. Then he knew that wasn't right because Aunt Bessie had given him a hint, and the hint was that the name of his present began with B.

Bat, ball, box, bank. Danny thought of all the words he knew that began with B. None of them sounded just right for a surprise combination birthday present. Beaver, bird, bunny. Danny liked animals better than anything in the world. Somehow he did not think his present was going to be a bird or a beaver or a bunny.

His eyes moved on along the valley to Aunt Bessie's vegetable garden. There he saw Barnacle Bland, the scarecrow. B! B! Barnacle Bland was dressed in a sailor suit and a high top hat. He was the finest scarecrow in all the world, and both of his names began with B. But of course Danny knew that Barnacle Bland was not going to be his surprise combination birthday present.

Just then Uncle Bill's farm truck rumbled and rattled across the cornfield. The truck was piled high with corn, and right on top of all the sliding, shining, golden ears was something black. Danny stared and stared at that black thing, and for a minute he even forgot about his birthday. Uncle Bill stopped the truck by the corncrib and got out. Then he reached up and lifted down the black thing. It stretched itself and walked over to the old stone hitching post and clambered up on top of it. Danny laughed out loud. The black thing was only Inky, Uncle Bill's cat! Inky was so old and stiff that whenever she climbed up on the hitching post she had to miaow and miaow for Uncle Bill or Aunt Bessie when she wanted to come down.

Right now Inky curled herself up for a sun bath on the hitching post and Uncle Bill unloaded his corn. When he was finished he went to the cab of the truck and took out two, four, six, SEVEN big orange pumpkins! Then he put them in a line on the stone wall by the barnyard. When Danny saw them he grinned like a jack-o'-lantern himself. Uncle Bill made the best pumpkin faces and Aunt Bessie made the best pumpkin pie in the whole world, but that wasn't all. Now that Danny saw those seven big round pumpkins he remembered another hint about his surprise combination birthday present.

You had to be seven, not three or five or even six, but seven years old to own it!

Aunt Bessie and Uncle Bill had come over after

supper last Monday to talk to Mother and Father about Danny's birthday. Danny knew it was about that, because before they left, Aunt Bessie came up to kiss him good night and told him so.

"It's all settled and it begins with a B," she said, and then she had given him the other hint. "We've all just agreed that seven years old is plenty big and grown up enough for our surprise combination birthday present."

"Tell me more!" Danny said. He hugged her so close that he could smell the perfume of wild grapes and spices that were still in her hair from jelly making. "Tell me more or I'll bust."

Aunt Bessie had just laughed in the darkness. She laughed the slow, low, pigeon cote rumble of a laugh that always made Danny feel cozy. But she wouldn't tell him anything more. She wouldn't say a word except that his surprise combination birthday present began with a B. AND that when he was seven he would be big enough and grown up enough to own it.

Right now Danny jumped out of his leaf fort and started down the hill. He took great long striding steps and he felt big enough for anything. For a boat, for a bear, for a big brass band.

Danny reached the bottom of the hill when Mike and Tad flashed past him on their bicycles. "Hi, slow-poke!" Mike said, waving a free hand. "Is this as far as you've gone?"

"Hi," Tad said, and for a moment he stood up with both feet in the saddle. "If you'd just learn to bike well you could zoom home."

Then the two big boys put both hands on their handle bars and both feet on their pedals and raced each other along the flat stretch of the lane toward home. Danny stood still and stared after them. His heart sank as though someone had pushed it down like a bicycle pedal. Finally he began to walk again, only now he took slow, sad, heavy steps. Even a little horned snail on the stone wall beside him moved faster than he did.

Danny walked so slowly that he stopped. He stopped because as the big boys biked out of sight he was sure his surprise combination birthday present was going to be a bicycle. Why, way back before school last August, Father had even taken him down to the store to look at a bicycle. Father and the big boys had gone all over it and said what a fine bike it was. Then when they went home Danny had had a lesson in bicycle riding, and how he had hated it! Mother and Father, the two big boys, and five-year-old Sally, who was the baby of the family, had all stood and watched while Danny tried riding Mike's bicycle.

Danny had fallen twice, and as soon as the big boys knew he wasn't hurt they had roared with laughter. Then Mother and Father had lifted Sally onto Tad's bike. Sally was so small that her feet hardly touched the pedals, but she was much quicker at learning than Danny.

Well, finally Danny had learned, sort of. But even when he could get off without falling and get on with only one person helping, he didn't like it. Bicycling was either a hot sticky push uphill or a cold scary rush downhill, Danny thought. And he knew he did not want a bicycle of his own for his surprise combination birthday present.

Danny began to walk again. Now he didn't hear the rustle of the leaves or smell the peppery autumn smell of bayberries by the old stone wall. He just walked along slowly with his head down. He didn't even look up when Old Siwash, Uncle Bill's mule, put his long neck over the wall, hoping for sugar or a carrot.

"Danny, Danny. Aren't you coming to see us?" When Danny heard that he turned. There was Aunt Bessie standing beside the stone hitching post, stroking Inky.

So Danny went over and Aunt Bessie lifted Inky down and they all went into the kitchen together. Aunt Bessie gave Inky a bowl of milk. Then she gave Danny a glass of milk and three of the chewy brown butternut cookies she had just taken out of the oven. When Danny was finished she let him mix a pailful of corn meal and skim milk for the piglets. Usually

Danny liked mixing big beautifully sloshy pailfuls of pig food better than anything. But today he was thinking so hard about his surprise combination present he didn't really enjoy it.

Even when he and Aunt Bessie carried the pail out to the pigpen his mind stayed on bicycles. The five little pigs came running, grunting and squealing for their food. Bratso and Fatso, the biggest piglets came first. Then Waltz and Schmaltz, the next biggest and finally Half Pint, the runt. Half Pint tried so hard to get his share that he put his front feet in the trough. But Danny didn't say a word.

"What's the matter, Danny?" Aunt Bessie said finally. "Did something go wrong at school?"

"School?" Danny said, and the morning seemed as long ago as Christmas. "School? No, I was just wondering——"

"About your birthday present?" Aunt Bessie asked. Danny looked away from her, and she beamed down at him, pleased with herself for guessing. "I know just how you feel. I remember how I felt just before my tenth birthday. I knew my family were going to give me a bicycle and I thought I couldn't stand waiting. But the day finally came, and the bike seemed better than ever because I'd waited for so long."

"Yes," Danny said, and suddenly his throat felt as dry as though he'd swallowed a pine cone. "Well, thanks for the cookies, and now I guess I'd better go home."

He walked the short way down the lane very, very slowly, and now he was more certain than ever that his surprise combination present was going to be a bicycle.

Danny's family were already at supper by the time he reached home. Danny washed his hands and brushed his hair. When he pulled out his chair he saw that Father had his big gold watch on the table in front of him. "You're late," Father said, and snapped the watch back into his pocket. "Half an hour late."

" 'Scuse me," Danny said, and began to eat his stew. "I stopped in at Aunt Bessie's and helped her feed the piglets."

"Did you feed your own ducks?" Father asked. "Have they been fed since morning?"

"N-no," Danny said, and felt as though he'd swallowed two pine cones. "No. But I'll feed them after supper."

It was late and dark by the time they had all finished supper. From the kitchen window Danny couldn't even see the barn where the ducks lived. He put bread scraps and carrots into his special basket and pulled on his sweater. Then as he started out into the darkness he decided he would like some company.

"Sally," he called back. "Sally, would you like to go with me? You know you love to feed the ducks."

But Sally was already in her pajamas, brushing her teeth for bed.

"How about one of you?" Danny said to his two big brothers.

"Can't," Mike said, and started up the stairs two steps at a time. "Homework."

"Can't," Tad said, and headed for the cellar. "I have to finish the jack-o'-lantern I'm making for the school party."

"I'll go," said Mother, "as soon as I've finished the dishes."

"I'll help," said Danny and soon they were on their way. Danny carried Mother's big red flashlight. The light made the barn seem even nicer than it was in the daytime. Danny was in no hurry to leave.

"The ducks are neat," he said as they watched the white one settle down in her straw bed for the night. "If I had three more I'd be able to start a duck farm."

Just then Father came out of the dark, unused side of the barn. "Plenty of room," Father said to Mother, but Danny was so busy watching the two gray ducks that he didn't hear him or see him.

"It's going to be clear and cold tomorrow." Father spoke louder, and this time Danny heard him and jumped like a startled chipmunk. "It'll be a perfect day for Halloween."

126

They all walked down to the house together. Then when Danny started upstairs to bed Mother and Father sat down in front of the living-room fire.

"Danny does love animals," Mother said. Danny knew he ought not to be listening, but somehow his feet didn't move along the upstairs hall.

"That's —true —enough!" Father said. Danny could tell from the sound of his voice that he was lighting his pipe as he spoke. "I almost wish we'd bought him rabbits or guinea pigs for his birthday. Still, you and Bessie were both sure seven was grown up enough for . . ."

Danny never heard for what. Just then Mike and Tad clattered through the hall and he had to go on to his own little bedroom. He undressed quickly and turned off the light. As he put his toes down between the clean, icy sheets he was sure, cold-clammy sure, about the bicycle.

The next morning when Danny woke up he could see that Father had been right about the weather. It was so cold that the fields were still quilted with frost and so clear that Danny could see a thin blue curl of wood smoke going up from Uncle Bill's chimney.

Danny put his Indian suit over his school clothes and dashed downstairs for breakfast. Mother must have cooked something extra special, because the house smelled sweet and spicy and just right for Halloween.

"Many happy returns, Danny boy," Mother said. "And happy Halloween. I hope you have a lovely day and that you like being seven."

"Thanks," Danny said, "and Miss Parker told us to wear our costumes to school, so can I keep on my Indian suit?"

"Of course," Mother said. "But now eat your breakfast."

So Danny ate country sausage and spiced apple fritters. As he ate he felt much more cheerful than he had last night. Perhaps he had guessed wrong about getting a bicycle. Or perhaps if he had guessed right, the grownups would let him sell it. Then he could buy chickens or guinea pigs or loads more ducks.

It was a good day at school and a good day at home. By half-past four Danny knew he liked being seven. He had walked home quickly and without stopping. He had fed his ducks without being reminded. He had remembered to bring home the pumpkin card he had made at school for Mother and Father at the Halloween party. And he still had enough time left so that he could make another card to take to Uncle Bill and Aunt Bessie.

Danny had just started drawing when Sally bounced into his room in the rabbit suit that the big boys and Danny himself had worn when they were little. "Look at me!" Sally said. "I can hop like a rabbit."

"Neat," Danny said, and began coloring. "Fine!"

"Danny, darling, are you coming?" Mother put her head around the door just as Danny drew in some fine jagged pumpkin teeth. "I promised Aunt Bessie that Sally and I'd drive over early so that I could help with supper. Father's going straight from work, and the big boys are going to bicycle."

"I'll walk," Danny said, because he seemed to walk faster now he was seven. "It won't take me two minutes."

So Mother and Sally drove off and Danny went on with his drawing. For a few minutes there wasn't any sound in the house except the tick of the big hall clock. Then as Mike and Tad began to dress for the party, the house rang with bumps and scuffles and laughs and giggles.

Last week Mother had taken all four children down to the store to choose Halloween masks. Tad had picked out a devil mask. Mike had chosen a rhino's face with one yellow tusk. Neither of the big boys would tell a soul what he was going to be at the Halloween-birthday party. Even now Danny couldn't tell from the sounds whether they were going to be scary or funny.

Just then the front door slammed. The next instant the house was tick-tock quiet again. So Danny knew he wouldn't find out until he went to the party. He finished his pumpkin card and put on the ghost mask he had chosen. The ghost mask looked fine above the Indian suit, but when Danny tried to put on his feather headdress above that it didn't fit.

For a minute Danny didn't know what to do, and then he had a really good idea. He had two long turkey feathers that Aunt Bessie had given him. If he could just fasten those to his head with string, they'd be better than his headdress. He looked in his treasure chest and he looked in back of the bookcase. He looked in Sally's room and he looked in the kitchen. Then he remembered that he had seen the turkey feathers in the croquet box on the front porch.

The feathers were still there. When Danny tied them on to the back of his head he looked like a very ghostly Indian.

He left the house and hurried along the lane toward Uncle Bill's and Aunt Bessie's. He could just see the seven jack-o'-lanterns lighting the way to the back door before he remembered his cards. He turned right around and ran back home to get them. He was sure—well, almost sure—he'd left the cards on his bureau. They weren't there and he finally found them under his schoolbooks, which was where he had put them in the first place.

He started off again and now it was very dark out and much colder. Danny shivered inside his Indian suit and scuttled along the side of the lane as fast as he could go. The leaves rustled at his feet, but some-

how it wasn't the same cheerful sound that it was in the daylight. There were other noises too. There were creakings and snappings behind the stone wall. And overhead there was the cold, lonely wail of the wind blowing through the telephone wires.

Danny pushed his cards into his pockets and ran until he had to stop for breath. He had reached Uncle Bill's lawn by that time. He walked more and more slowly while his heart thumped faster and faster. Danny wasn't scared, of course. It was just that the bushes looked so big and black in the darkness. If the twins had put on scary costumes and were going to jump out at him, this was where they would do it.

The farmhouse curtains were drawn and there was no light except from the jack-o'-lanterns. The jack-o'-lanterns were set out wide apart from each other. Danny knew from last year that they made a path around the house to the back door.

He went so close to the first jack-o'-lantern that he could see the pumpkin seeds Uncle Bill had used for teeth. He touched the cold round shell of the pumpkin for luck. Then he hurried through the deep, black shadows to the next one. He stood still for a second, as though he were playing Red Light-Green Light. Then he scurried on to the third pumpkin.

By the time Danny reached the sixth pumpkin he was in the pitch blackness between the barn and the woodshed. He could see the seventh and biggest jack-o'-lantern quite a long way ahead of him. He guessed it was on top of the old stone hitching post by the kitchen door and took one step toward it. He took two steps, and then a queer thing happened!

One minute that big bright grin was straight ahead of him. Then there was a thud and the grin flickered out into darkness.

Danny took two steps backward, and his heart thumped faster than ever. He stared over to where the grin had been and then he saw the eyes. They were cold, round, greeny eyes. They stared down at him from where the jack-o'-lantern had been only a second before.

For an instant Danny was scared. So scared that his breath stopped and his hair prickled up under his Indian feathers. Then there was a loud angry "Miaow" and Danny started to breathe again. It was only Inky! Inky had knocked over the pumpkin face when she'd clambered up onto her favorite seat on top of the hitching post.

"Here, Inky, here, puss!" Danny said. Just then the barn door behind him began to open.

Danny didn't hear the door or see the door, but by the thin sliver of light that came through it he saw more of Inky. Inky's back was arched. She was frightened and angry and spitting. Danny stared. Then he saw why Inky was frightened! He saw teeth and a long gray face just below Inky. The body, if there was one, was still lost in shadows.

When Danny saw that face his skin crawled. He didn't know whether it was a spook, or a wild beast, or a big boy playing tricks. He didn't care, either. No matter what it was, Danny knew he didn't like it. He wanted to run into Uncle Bill's house or hide his eyes and yell for Mother. Then, as Inky miaowed again, he knew he couldn't! Inky's leg was so stiff that she couldn't get off the hitching post unless someone helped her.

Danny gave an Indian war whoop to make himself feel braver. Then he rushed toward the hitching post. At the same time the kitchen door in front of him opened wide. In that sudden burst of light Danny saw everything. He saw the gray face had long, long ears and that now the teeth were covered by soft furry lips. It wasn't a spook, or a wild beast, or a mean boy trying to scare Inky. It was a small gray donkey!

Aunt Bessie and Uncle Bill, Mother and Sally and Father were all out of the kitchen door by that time, and someone shouted, "Happy Birthday, Danny! The burro is your surprise combination birthday present beginning with B!"

Aunt Bessie lifted Inky down from the hitching post, and Inky rushed off toward the barn just as Tad and Mike came out of it. Tad was dressed in Barnacle Bland's clothes and the devil mask. Mike was dressed in an old worn-out evening dress with the rhino's face on top of that.

"Boys!" Father said. "You promised me there wouldn't be any scaring——"

"There wasn't. By us, anyway," Tad said, and then Father lifted Danny onto the donkey's warm furry back.

Danny touched the neat black cross on the donkey's shoulders. He patted his neck and picked up the reins that Father gave him. Uncle Bill turned on the yard light, and Danny rode the little donkey three times all the way around the barnyard.

"The burro's name is Lucky," Aunt Bessie said, when Danny stopped to give Sally a ride. "Do you really like him?"

"L-like him!" Danny said, and he was so excited and happy his words were shaky.

Just then Lucky reached out and nibbled at the edge of the Halloween cards that were still in Danny's pocket. Danny gave the cards away. He found a little corn candy in the bottom of his pocket and gave that to Lucky. The donkey ate it all up and nudged Danny's shoulder for more.

Everybody laughed when they saw that, and Aunt Bessie said: "Then everyone's pleased except Inky. She will be when you take Lucky back to live in your own barn. Inky was jealous when we tied Lucky to her hitching post."

When Danny heard that, he told them how he'd first seen the lighted pumpkin and then Inky's eyes and Lucky's teeth. He told them just how scared he'd been when he knew he'd have to rescue Inky.

"Supper's ready!" Aunt Bessie said, when Danny had finished his story. "Who is hungry enough to eat birthday cake and pumpkin pie for dessert?"

"I am," Tad said.

"I am," Mike said.

"Me too," said Sally, and they all trooped into the farmhouse.

Danny stayed behind long enough to make sure that Lucky was warm and cozy in one of Uncle Bill's empty stalls. When he finally turned away he saw that Father was waiting for him just outside the barn door.

"Now I know you're big enough!" Father said. He swung Danny up on his shoulders so that he was higher than the corncrib. "A boy that's ready to rescue a lame cat on Halloween is grown up enough and brave enough for a combination birthday present of a burro!"

THE
FLORIDA-PLYMOUTH
THANKSGIVING

From the minute Johnny Bemis stepped off the
Florida plane at the Boston airport nothing seemed
to be the way he had hoped and expected. The
weather was colder and windier. The country just beyond the airport was bleaker and barer and much,
much uglier. Even the people he saw around him
looked older and colder and more in a hurry than the
ones at home. Most unexpected of all, Johnny's
great-uncle Joel Bemis, whom Johnny had never seen

before, had called for him at the airport instead of his grandmother Bemis.

In one way, since Johnny had spent all of his ten years in Siesta Cove, Florida, where his father worked at the Jungle Gardens it wasn't strange that he was surprised on his first trip to Massachusetts. But in another way it was strange. Johnny's father had been born and brought up in Plymouth and had told him all about it. Ever since Johnny could remember he'd wanted to spend a real old-fashioned New England Thanksgiving like the ones in Dad's best stories. At last Johnny's wish had come true and here he was on the Monday before Thanksgiving driving to Plymouth to visit Granny Bemis for five whole days. The queer part was that instead of being thrilled and happy the way he'd expected to be, Johnny suddenly felt as lost and uneasy as a cat in a strange garret.

"We're nearly there," Great-Uncle Joel said, after a long and very silent drive. "Only two more miles."

Johnny perked up and looked out so as not to miss a single thing. After all, the reason why everyone at home had been so pleased when Granny Bemis had invited him North was because he, John-Winthrop Bemis III, was going to bring back descriptions, and pictures, and all sorts of odds and ends for an exhibit so that everybody in his grade at school would feel they had been to Plymouth too.

Mr. Bemis turned onto the shore road and suddenly Johnny saw something that did look familiar. "Uncle Joel! Uncle Joel!" he got out. "Isn't that little old summer house on the top of Plymouth Rock? Dad said when he was my age he and a friend of his got down below the summer house and climbed all over the Rock itself."

Mr. Bemis began to answer but at that moment the traffic light turned red and he braked the car to a sudden stop instead. Instantly Johnny jumped out of the car and headed toward Plymouth Rock. He wasn't feeling lost and queer any more but just plain thrilled because he was going to have a chance to climb all over Plymouth Rock just the way Dad had done. More than that, if he looked carefully he might even find a little piece of the Rock to take home to show Miss Perla, his teacher, and the rest of the fifth grade.

Johnny hadn't counted on Great-Uncle Joel. In no time flat the old gentleman had him by the arm and hauled him back to the car. "I didn't mean any harm," Johnny began, "I thought you stopped on purpose so I could get a real good look at the Rock."

"Fiddlesticks!" Great-Uncle Joel said. As he started the car again, it was clear he didn't believe a word Johnny had said. "From now on, young man, I'll trouble you to behave yourself. I thought I'd made it plain that the reason why I met you at the airport and why your great aunts have just moved into the house on Linden Street is because your grandmother Bemis is not well. She's not at all well and if she's bothered or disturbed in any way she may not even be able to come down to the Thanksgiving dinner on Thursday."

"I won't bother her," Johnny said, and craned his neck for another look at the unfamiliar waterfront. "Why I promised Mom I'd move around just as quiet as the new black panther in our Jungle Gardens back home. I was just hoping maybe I'd find a little bitty chip of Plymouth Rock to take to school."

Mr. Bemis' eyebrows lifted, but Johnny was too busy looking around him to notice. "Jeepers creepers, this is terrific!" he said. "All those white wooden houses and the little old streets. And when do I get to go on board the *Mayflower II*, Uncle Joel?"

"I don't know, I'm sure," Uncle Joel said. "As chairman of the Preservation of Landmarks and Antiquities Society I take no interest whatsoever in shams."

"Well, sometimes a rival attraction helps business," Johnny said. "Leastwise that's what Gaga Choiseaux, my mom's mom, said when the alligator farm started up across the road from our Jungle Gardens. And Gaga ought to know. She was in show business, real high-class vaudeville, before she got married."

Mr. Bemis snorted and started to speak, but Johnny didn't hear him. At that moment they pulled up in front of a big old-fashioned house on Linden Street and Johnny knew he had arrived at last. He jumped out of the car, and ran out up the brick walk toward the door with the big brass knocker on it that Dad said you could hear in China. Before Johnny reached it, the door opened and there were two tall, very erect old ladies looking down at him.

"Welcome to Plymouth, John-Winthrop Bemis," one lady said. "I am your great-aunt Maria and this is your great-aunt Jane. We're delighted to see you. And how is your father?"

"Pop's fine and so's Mom," Johnny said, when he had shaken hands with both the old ladies. "And how soon can I see Granny?"

"Presently dear, presently," Great-Aunt Jane said, and looked at him over her steel-rim spectacles. "But first you had better help Uncle Joel bring in your suitcase and then hang up your coat in this clothes-press where your father always hung his. Such a tall upstanding boy Winthrop was! Why he could reach that hook when he wasn't a day over seven."

Johnny reached for the hook and just made it even though he was ten years and three months. "Guess I'm real runty-like," he said and swung on the hook to prove that he'd reached it. "But Gaga says the runts often turn out to be pick of the litter."

"Mm? Indeed? I don't quite understand . . ." Great-Aunt Jane began, when Great-Aunt Maria interrupted her. "That hook is to hang coats on, John-Winthrop," she said. "It is not a piece of gymnasium equipment. And now please hurry and fetch your bag so that Uncle Joel can put the car away."

The next few minutes were filled with so many orders and instructions that Johnny hardly had a chance to get in a question. And when he did, the great-aunts either didn't seem to understand him at all or their answers were discouraging. No, Granny wasn't well enough to come downstairs until Thanksgiving Day. No, there weren't any boy or girl cousins his age living in the neighborhood. No, no one had found any arrowheads like the ones Dad had collected around Plymouth for many years and Johnny was most unlikely to find any.

By the time the great-aunts left Johnny alone in the prim white-curtained bedroom which they said had been his father's, he felt even colder and stranger and more lost then he had when he'd first arrived. He shivered and washed his hands, just to get some part of him into good hot water. As he washed he saw his face in the mirror and slicked down his hair and stuck out his jaw so as to look more like his father. It was not very successful because Johnny's hair was dark and curly and his father's was blond and straight. Still it made Johnny feel better to think about his father. He remembered all of Dad's stories about Plymouth Thanksgivings and that made him glad all over again he was going to have one himself. He put his hand in his pocket and found the two dollars Gaga had given him at the airport and felt better than ever. Of course this trip was going to be a honey even if he couldn't climb over Plymouth Rock or maybe get to go on the *Mayflower*. With Gaga's present he'd be able to buy a lot of things for an exhibit to show Miss Perla and the other kids at school.

Johnny made sure his money was safe and went off to find Granny Bemis' bedroom. Almost all of Dad's best Plymouth stories had Granny in them and Johnny could hardly wait to see her again. She'd come down to visit them in Florida when Johnny was five. That was so long ago he could hardly remember her but this time would be different. He had half run, half slid over the waxy floor to what he was sure must be the door of Granny's room, when he saw that the two great-aunts were waiting for him.

"Just pay your grandmother a very brief visit, John-Winthrop," Great-Aunt Maria told him. "Just stay with her for a very few minutes. She must save her strength for Thanksgiving Day."

"Yes, indeed," Great-Aunt Jane said. "And be sure, dear, that you try to speak very, very clearly. Your

Grandmother Bemis isn't used to a southern accent, and she may not understand you."

It went through Johnny's mind to say that Granny seemed to have understood O.K. when she'd visited them at Siesta Cove. At that moment the great-aunts opened the door to Granny's room and Johnny forgot all about it. Granny Bemis looked even older and smaller than the way he remembered her, but her hug and her laugh were just the same and made Johnny feel wonderful. Granny asked after Mom and Dad and Gaga Choiseaux and the Jungle Gardens. Johnny told her everything he could think of. He was just beginning to tell her about his plan for a Plymouth exhibit when the great-aunts said Granny was tired and it was time for him to leave.

"But Granny didn't look tired," Johnny said, when they were once more out in the hall. "And Gaga, that's my other granny, says she only gets feeling tired when she's all by her lonesome."

The Great Aunts started to answer but just then a new, cheerful voice called up from downstairs. The great-aunts hurried down, taking Johnny with them.

"Sarah, this is Winthrop's boy," Aunt Jane said when they reached the living room. "His name is John-Winthrop Bemis, though he doesn't look in the least like any of the Winthrops or the Bemises."

"John-Winthrop, say how do you do to your cousin Sarah Hodges," Great-Aunt Maria said. "She is your father's first cousin and one of the very busiest women in Plymouth. It was extremely good of her to take the time away from her office to come over to see you."

Johnny shook hands with a short stocky little lady in a thick tweed suit. She was younger than the great-aunts but older than Mom and not nearly so pretty. For a minute Johnny was confused, but then he realized that she and her brother Bob were the cousins who been Dad's special pals when he was a boy in Plymouth. "You-all must be Squash," he said, and as Great-Aunt Jane gasped, he corrected himself, "Cousin Sarah, ma'am. Dad's told me all about how you and he and Bob, Cousin Bob, I mean, let out the Thanksgiving turkey and you all were caught holding the sack. And you didn't tell on any of 'em."

"I don't follow what he's saying," Great-Aunt Jane began, but Cousin Sarah didn't notice her.

"Good!" she said, and grinned at Johnny. "You must call me Cousin Squash if you know that story. But what I really came over for was to ask if you'd like to help me decorate the table on Thursday. Thanksgiving dinner will be late because Bob and some of the rest of the family can't get here ahead of time. We might even have a chance to do a little sight-seeing early in the afternoon."

"I'd like that mighty fine," Johnny said, and began to tell her about the Plymouth exhibit he wanted to take back to Florida.

At that, Great-Uncle Joel put down the *Old Colony Memorial* which he had been reading and glared at Johnny. "Sarah, the boy's not just a Florida cracker but a fire cracker to boot. Why, when I stopped the car for a light he dashed out to chip off a piece of Plymouth Rock."

"But I wasn't going to chip off anything!" Johnny tried to explain all over and Cousin Squash nodded.

"I believe you," she said as she moved toward the door. "When I see you on Thursday I'll want to hear more about it and about all the Plymouth adventures you have in the meantime. So don't forget anything. And give my love to Granny Bemis. My, she must be happy to have a boy in the house again."

Maybe Granny Bemis was happy to have a boy around but even by Thursday morning Johnny hadn't had much chance of finding out. He was only allowed to see Granny for a few minutes each day and one or both of the great-aunts stayed right there in the bedroom with him.

As for Plymouth adventures, Johnny hadn't had any. Not, that is, unless you counted the times he'd goofed something and both the great-aunts and Great-Uncle Joel had pointed out that his father would have done better. There was the time early Tuesday morning when Uncle Joel had taken him birding along the shore and Johnny had been so cold and hungry he'd pleaded to go home. Then Tuesday evening they'd sent him out to the barn for a piece of wire and Johnny had gotten lost and sort of scared and had come back without it. But worst of all was the time the great-aunts had taken him to an exhibition of old maps at the Preservation of Landmarks and Antiquities Society. Johnny had waited around for ages and then scuttled off down Main Street without telling them he was leaving. He'd gone straight to a souvenir shop and spent most of Gaga's money on a model of the *Mayflower*. The great-aunts got back to Linden Street before he did, even though they'd spent the best part of an hour searching for him. "And your father was such a dependable boy," Great-Aunt Maria had said. "One could always trust Winthrop to say where he was going."

Uncle Joel had reached for the model of the *Mayflower*. "Typical tourist trinket," he said, and turned it upside down to show Johnny the words "Made in Newark, N.J." at the bottom of it. "No real connection with Plymouth whatsoever."

At the time, Johnny had felt he'd wasted his money. But right now, early on Thanksgiving afternoon when he was alone in the neat front parlor, where the great-aunts had sent him to get him out from underfoot in the kitchen, he wasn't so sure. Maybe if you didn't come from Plymouth you wouldn't mind its being made in Newark. Anyway it was the only thing besides a few post cards that he'd been able to get for his exhibit.

At that moment Cousin Squash came into the room. Johnny tried to hide the model of the *Mayflower* under a sofa pillow, but Cousin Squash was too quick for him. "What difference does that make?" she said, when Johnny showed her that it was made in Newark. "Tomorrow when Bob's here he'll be able to take you on board the *Mayflower II* before you have to go to the airport and you can see for yourself if it's a good copy. I'd love to take you but I'll have to be at the office."

They went out of doors and now, with a heavy sweater on, which Cousin Squash had brought over for him, Johnny didn't feel cold a bit. He stopped worrying, too, about not being like Dad and about his exhibition. Now that he knew he was going to see the *Mayflower II* he was much too interested in hearing everything that Cousin Squash told him about it to worry at all.

Cousin Squash led the way down a narrow lane behind Granny's barn and turned off onto a steep hilly field where a few stalks of dried corn were still standing. "Indian corn," Cousin Squash said and pulled back the papery husk from the tawny red and brown kernels. "I guess your father told you how the Indians saved the Pilgrims from starving by teaching them to plant their corn with fish heads for fertilizer. And about Squanto, the Indian who walked down to the beach when they landed and said, 'Welcome white man'?"

"Yes. Yes, ma'am," Johnny said, but now, at the top of the hill looking out over the cold gray water of Plymouth Bay, he was thinking of something else that Dad had told him. "This is it!" he burst out, and for the first time since he'd arrived something looked the way he'd expected it to from Dad's stories. "This is the hill you and Cousin Bob and my dad used to camp out on. You called it Merrymount after that place where everybody danced and had fun and didn't worry about being good Pilgrims."

"Merrymount is right!" Cousin Squash beamed at Johnny. "And this is where I got my nickname Squash, because one of the Squire boys had dressed up a hollowed-out squash with an old sheet and I thought it was the ghost of Elder Brewster."

"Dad said he was scared silly too!" Johnny remembered the story so well he almost felt as though he had been there himself.

"We all were," Cousin Squash said. "But the worst part of it was when I tried to run away I tripped and dropped my arrowhead collection. Bob and Win got it back for me later but that night I thought it was lost for good and I was heartbroken. Somehow those little stone arrows that you could see and touch were the first things that ever made history seem real to me or the least bit exciting."

"Golly, I know how you felt," Johnny said. "I wanted to find some arrowheads for my exhibit, but the great-aunts told me there weren't any left. I thought maybe they were wrong but I guess they weren't because I haven't seen a smitch of one since I've been here."

"What a shame," Cousin Squash said. "Because arrowheads would be just right for your exhibit. And I think the exhibit is a great idea."

"So did Mom and Miss Perla," Johnny said as they started downhill. "But Great-Uncle Joel and the great-aunts don't think it's any good at all."

"I bet Granny Bemis thinks it's wonderful!" Cousin Squash said. She sounded so sure of it that Johnny told her how he hadn't had a chance to visit alone with Granny long enough to find out. Cousin Squash seemed so interested that he went on to tell her how both the great-aunts and Great-Uncle Joel made him feel as though he were something out of a zoo because he didn't look or talk or act the way they remembered his father had when he was ten.

"The whole trip's been sort of queer," Johnny ended up. "It's bad enough not getting anything much for my exhibit but it's worse not finding anything until just now on the top of the hill that was the way that Dad said it would be."

"Much worse," Cousin Squash said and led the way toward a small open shed. The shed was filled with all sizes and shapes of gourds and squash and pumpkins. As soon as Johnny saw them he knew that the littlest ones and the Indian corn would be just right for his exhibit.

"Help yourself," Cousin Squash said, and searched around the shed like a short-legged and very excited hound. "John Squire, who owns this place, said we could have as many as we want. So it's really a matter of picking out as many as we'll be able to carry for your exhibit and the table decorations."

"Couldn't we come back in a car?" Johnny asked as Cousin Squash loaded him up with what seemed like a ton of vegetables.

"Won't be time," she said, and looked regretfully at one odd-shaped gourd in the corner. "As it is, I'm going to have to leave you at the Harlow House while I drive back to decorate the table and call for Bob at the airport. Somehow or other, you and I'll have to be all dressed up and ready for Thanksgiving dinner at seven."

"I'll be ready!" Johnny said. "I'm half starved now. But tell me about the Harlow House. Is it like the Antiquarian and Preservation of Landmarks Society?"

"Not a bit. It's a very old house run by a friend of mine who understands things like your exhibit and my arrowhead collection. If you ask her, she'll let you try spinning and carding yourself. And maybe give you some samples for your exhibit."

"No!" Johnny stopped short on the brick path leading to Granny's and stared at Cousin Squash. "I reckon you're kidding?"

"I am not," Cousin Squash said. "It's really fun and Rosie Howland's opening it up specially for us."

"Yippee!" Johnny was so excited that he tried to jump, run, and give the Rebel yell, which Gaga had taught him, all at the same time. He dropped half of his load instead, and two crookneck squashes cracked open on the brick wall. He stared down at them and for once he couldn't think of a single word to say. They were ones that Cousin Squash had counted on for the table. Now she'd have to go back for others and there wouldn't be time to go to the Harlow House or get anything more for his exhibit. He waited, shivering, for Cousin Squash to say so or to laugh and tell him that his father had never been such a butterfingers.

Neither thing happened. Cousin Squash was down on her hands and knees picking up the broken bits and pieces. "Take the good ones round to the back door," she said. "And meet me in the car. I don't much like crookneck squash anyway."

Minutes later, when they were driving off in the car, Johnny tried to tell Cousin Squash he was sorry

he'd been so clumsy. She wouldn't listen to him. "Ever since that time on Merrymount I've hated squash," she said. "Except just once when your dad and Bob fixed an acorn squash for me."

"Tell me about it," Johnny said, but by then they had reached the Harlow House and there wasn't time.

The next two hours passed in a flash. Mrs. Howland was a tall, gray-haired lady dressed in a Pilgrim costume. She looked a little like Great-Aunt Jane but she acted more like Miss Perla, who was the nicest teacher Johnny had ever had. She showed him how the big open fireplace in the kitchen was used for cooking. She explained how the carding comb was used to straighten out the sheep's wool before spinning it into thread and weaving it into coarse cloth. She even let Johnny try carding and spinning himself before she showed him how the Pilgrims made candles scented with bayberries, how they made soup out of wood ashes and fat, and how they used the roots and berries they found right around Plymouth to make dyes. Best of all, Mrs. Howland gave Johnny little samples of newly carded wool, of flaxen thread, bayberries, and all sorts of other things to use in his exhibit.

By the time Mrs. Howland drove Johnny to Linden Street, Johnny's pockets were so full that he had to hold the package of postal cards of every room in the Harlow House in his hands. "Thanks. Thanks a million," Johnny said when they reached Linden Street. "This was great."

"You're welcome," Mrs. Howland said, as she drove off. "But you really ought to thank your cousin Sarah. It was all her idea."

"Yes, ma'am. I surely will," Johnny said. "Right away quick."

The minute Johnny was inside the house he had to think about something else. The front parlor was crowded with grownups who were clustered around Granny Bemis who sat, like a little queen, at the far end of the room. "Goody, Granny's downstairs." Johnny started toward her but Great-Aunt Maria collared him. "John-Winthrop! Your clothes. Your hands. You're filthy. Go upstairs and get clean and changed at once!"

Johnny went. And even with taking out time to spread out all the things for his exhibit on the old-fashioned dark-wood dresser he was very quick indeed.

He gave his hair a last slicking down and hurried back to the front parlor. There were people so thick around Granny he couldn't see her. And the people were all old, some of them even looked older than the great-aunts. When they spoke to Johnny they all either laughed at his accent or said he didn't look like his father.

Johnny edged back to the hallway looking for

Cousin Squash, but she was nowhere in sight. Just then Great-Uncle Joel, who had his back to Johnny, took out his big gold watch, opened it again, and shut it with a snap. "I was right," he said. "I knew Robert's plane would be late. They're never on time coming in from Chicago."

When Johnny heard that he moved quickly and quietly toward the front door. Cousin Squash had wanted that strange-shaped gourd in the corner of the shed. She'd probably wanted it more than ever after Johnny had broken the crooknecks. And right now while the grownups were talking, he was going to get it for her!

Johnny reached the door without being seen and looked up at the big old-fashioned clothespress for his windbreaker. He remembered that he'd left it upstairs and knew that he couldn't get it without someone asking him where he was going. He didn't want that to happen, so he slipped out and started to run as fast as he could along the narrow road toward the shed.

It was colder out than Johnny had expected and much, much darker. Once he was beyond the lights of the house, it was so black that he had to slow down a little for fear he'd fall or go past the shed. His teeth chattered now he wasn't running but at least his eyes were getting used to the darkness. By the time he reached the shed the moon came out from behind a cloud and he could see quite plainly. The harvest moon, Johnny thought, and as he looked up at the outline of the hill he gasped with surprise at how strange it looked in the moonlight. Dad saw the hill looking like that, Johnny thought. And so did my grandfather and his father before that, all the way back to the boys who lived here at the time of the Pilgrims. Squanto and the other Indians saw it too. And probably they were surprised and sort of, but not really, scared at how high and dark and strange it looks, just the way I was.

Johnny ducked in to the shed and as he began to pick out the gourds and squash, he forgot about the hilltop. He only knew that his hands were stiff and clumsy with cold and that he didn't have so much as a paper sack to carry things in. He found the gourd that Cousin Squash had wanted in the corner and buttoned it under his jacket. He picked up two or three others when he heard a noise beyond him. It was a loud scrabbling noise and it scared Johnny so that the hair on the back of his neck prickled and for a minute he couldn't move. Then he moved so fast that he dropped half of his gourds, but he didn't wait to pick them up. He just ran out of the shed and back up the narrow road without waiting for anything.

By the time Johnny had to stop for breath he could see the lights in Grandma Bemis' house and he knew he'd been silly to run from the shed. It was just a rat.

A little old no-count rat, Johnny told himself, and made sure that the gourd was still safely buttoned under his jacket. He had that and some little ones he'd put in his pocket, but that was all. He hurried on and now the exciting, happy, being-a-part-of-something feelings that had come over him when he'd first seen the hill in the moonlight were all gone. He was so cold that he couldn't think about anything except getting inside. He opened the door and then stood blinking in the sudden brightness from the dining room. The grownups were all seated. And there at the far end of the table Grandma Bemis was talking to a tall man who must be Cousin Bob Hodges.

Johnny wanted to run, to hide, most of all to just sink through the floor so that nobody would see him. It was too late. They'd all heard him come in and now every head was turned toward him and nobody spoke until Great-Uncle Joel brought out his watch. "The boy is fifteen minutes later than anybody else," he said. "When I was young, that would have meant no dinner."

Johnny saw that there was an empty place next to Cousin Squash and started toward it. If he could just slip into it without having to say anything or to explain, it would be wonderful. But even before Johnny was halfway he knew that first Mom and Gaga would want him to go and tell Granny Bemis he was sorry he was late. Somehow he made it and bent toward her, still shivering and hanging on to the gourd. "I'm sure enough sorry, Granny. Ma'am," he said, and because it was thinking of Mom and Gaga that had made him go forward, his speech was more southern than ever without his knowing it. "I aimed to get this squash for Cousin Sarah and I reckon it took longer going down to that shed in the dark than I'd 'spected."

"That's all right, Johnny," Granny said. "I think it was splendid of you to go after it and I hope you found some small ones for your exhibit." Johnny was so surprised at not being scolded and at Granny Bemis' having heard about his exhibit he wasn't quite sure of what happened next. Cousin Bob reached for the gourd before Johnny dropped it, shook hands, and led him back to the place beside Cousin Squash.

"First Johnny's going to have one whale of a dinner," Cousin Bob said. As he spoke, people stopped looking at Johnny as though he were something in the Jungle Gardens and began to eat again and talk to one another. "And after that I'd like to hear more about his trip down to Squires' shed in the dark."

"Thank you, Johnny," Cousin Squash said and put the gourd right in the middle of the table in front of all the others. "It's just the one I wanted."

Johnny nodded, but his mouth was so full of roast turkey and cranberry sauce that it was quite a while before he could say anything at all. Then when he'd finished everything and topped it off with two pieces of Great-Aunt Jane's pumpkin pie Cousin Squash turned to him. "You haven't looked at this," and nodded toward an acorn squash on the table in front of him. "It's like the one your dad and Bob fixed for me the Thanksgiving after I lost my arrowhead collection."

As Johnny reached for the squash, the top came off and he saw that it was neatly hollowed out and inside were six perfect white arrowheads. "For you," Cousin Squash said. "For your Florida-Plymouth Thanksgiving exhibit."

For a long time Johnny was too thrilled to speak. When the words finally came they weren't about the most important thing in his mind. That was that now his exhibit and the whole Thanksgiving visit were perfect. All he said was, "How come, Cousin Squash, how come Granny Bemis knew about my exhibit?"

"Because I told her," Cousin Squash said. "And she thought it was a wonderful idea, just the way I knew she would. You should have heard her scolding the great-aunts for not giving you a chance to tell her about it sooner. I give you my word they both looked scared silly when she finished with them."

Johnny laughed at the thought of the great-aunts being scared of Granny, who was only about half their size. "I wish I'd been here," he said, "only, only then I'd have missed getting your squash and feeling

like Dad and Grandfather Bemis and everybody back
to Squanto."

"Oh?" Cousin Sarah said. "Tell me about it."

So Johnny did. He told her everything that he had
seen and felt, even about being scared by the scrabbling of a rat. It wasn't until he was all through that
he realized that everyone at the table had been listening to him. He got red and itchy and then a strange
thing happened.

"Good boy!" Cousin Bob Hodge called out.
"Stout fella."

"He's really very like his father at that age," Great-
Aunt Maria said and Great-Aunt Jane added, "Yes,
he does take after the Bemises and the Winthrops."

"Johnny takes after both his father's *and* his mother's side of the family," Granny Bemis said, and
smiled at Johnny. "But what's much more important
he's himself and that means he's a sturdy New England Yankee as well as a brave and gallant southern
cavalier."

THE CHRISTMAS-
PRESENT RACE

The December wind whistled around the point of land called Blind Man's Beat. The small, old-fashioned iceboat tipped dangerously, but Derry Harris rolled her weight dexterously leeward to bring the light side down again. Tabs Harris held onto the tiller, his face wrinkled against the driving wind.

"Ready about!" he ordered. Then, as Derry flattened out, Tabs began to turn the little boat sharply around the point of the Beat. "Hard alee!" He snapped out the final command and the little *Frost*

King glided smoothly before the wind, on the black ice to the south of the Beat.

Derry took one look at the flight of green and red sails in front of them. Then she looked back at her twin brother and shook her head. "We gained some," she said, "but not enough."

Tabs Harris said nothing, but blew on one frosty hand while he guided his boat with the other. You couldn't expect even the best seamanship to make up the difference between a thirty-year-old crate like the *Frost King* and the new, trim, and shining ice-boats ahead of them. Still, Tabs had hoped that their choice of a tack around Blind Man's Beat would help. Now he watched the *Snow Queen*, the *Icicle*, and the *North Wind* glide silently into the dock of the Shrewsbury Yacht Club. Sails rattled as their owners brought them up into the wind. A moment later the sails were being taken down.

"I guess Mr. Robinson and Jed Lewis and Ted Kramer will be the cup defenders," Derry said, trying to keep her voice steady. Those were the owners of the first three boats.

Tabs nodded. "Well, that's fair enough," he said. "But I just wish . . ."

Derry nodded, and the wish hung between them, the stronger for being unspoken. They had both hoped with all their hearts that by some fluke they could manage to race in the All-Shrewsbury races that were to take place between the Shrewsbury Yacht Club and the Pine Point Club farther up the river.

"We'd do better in the All-Shrewsbury races," Derry said, as they swung into the harbor. "That course takes knowing the river as much as anything."

"Well, we won't have the chance," Tabs said grimly, and prepared to lower his sail just before they reached the club.

The following week it thawed and then rained and froze again. Tabs and Derry almost forgot about the iceboating because there was so much to be done for Christmas. They finished up the pipe rack they were making for Dad and the carved wooden box they were making for Mother. They bought presents for Aunt Louise and Uncle Ted, and the other relatives. They bought a small, silk-covered dictionary for Miss Mary Scarsborough, a muffler for old Robbie, her Scotch gardener, and a fine new collar for Laddie, the Scotch collie.

Miss Mary Scarsborough was a special friend of both Tabs and Derry. They had first come to know her two summers before, when their catboat had got stuck in the marsh just a few yards away from her lonely old house on the end of Blind Man's Beat. Tabs and Derry had gone ashore for help and had run into the sharp-tongued, erect old lady, who had liked them at sight, just as they had liked her.

The old Scotch gardener and the even older shepherd dog had helped them launch the boat. They had sailed away then, but on the next day, with more skillful seamanship, they had managed to put in at Miss Mary's unused old dock and had gone ashore to thank her.

From then on, the friendship had flourished. Once Miss Mary had invited them to a picnic on her point. Another time they had asked her out in their catboat. Miss Mary hadn't gone but she had seemed to be as pleased to be asked as a six-year-old child. "Miss Mary hasn't any folks of her own to look after her," Derry said that day, as they tacked away from the Beat. "That's why she likes us so much."

Tabs never wasted words, but he nodded his head and it was plain that he agreed.

When it came to Christmas time it was clear that Miss Mary Scarsborough was right up with Aunt Louise and Uncle Ted near the top of their list. The dictionary seemed a perfect present, and of course the other two members of her household came in for their presents too. But just a week before Christmas they began to wonder how they could get them there. "Mother'll take us in the car," Derry said hopefully, but when they suggested it to Mother she shook her head.

"I'm afraid there isn't a chance," she said, looking out of the window. "All this rain's frozen and the Blind Man's Beat road is absolutely impassable. Jeff

Andrews told me so this morning when I went down
to the store. Jeff can't even get Miss Scarsborough's
Christmas groceries out to her."

The twins went upstairs to Tabs' room for a coun-
cil. "There's no point sending our presents by mail,"
Derry said gloomily. "If Mother can't get there, the
postman can't."

Tabs looked out of the window without answering.
"We might wait," Derry suggested. "Perhaps just the
day before Christmas, Mother could get across."

"With Uncle Ted and Aunt Louise coming and
everything going on in the house?" Tabs said gloomily. "Not a chance. And I hate to think of Miss
Scarsborough's not having her mail and groceries.
She probably has plenty to eat, but it won't be Christmas things."

Derry moved over to the window beside him and
they both stared out over the frozen surface of the
Shrewsbury River. "We've just got to go," Tabs said
suddenly. "And we'd better go today."

"In the *Frost King!*" exclaimed Derry breathlessly.
Do you think we can make it?"

"We can try," said Tabs.

They pulled on their warmest clothes right then
and there and went down to collect Miss Mary's groceries and mail. When they reached the iceboat house
they found the place deserted except for Ben Van
Bergh, who had charge of the boats. "It's nasty sail-

ing," Ben warned them, when he had helped them get the *Frost King* off the wooden blocks and onto the ice. "The river's as uneven as a new-plowed field."

After they had their sails up, and Tabs had given them a push off, they understood what Ben meant. It certainly was nasty sailing. The wind was fitful and tricky and that was only the half of it. The river was bumpy and rough. In some places the wind had piled up little waves which had frozen into rough fatty-looking ridges. In other places there was a short fair space of black ice, bounded by a coast of white scum that looked treacherous.

"I think we'll keep as close to the Knoll as we can," Tabs said, "the way we did last time."

The Knoll was a high point of land on the south side of the Beat. If they couldn't go that way there was no other point of approach except along the marshes which bounded the Beat on the north, and the marshes were almost always impassable.

"We'll manage somehow," Derry said, and helped Tabs check the rigging and the rudder. They fastened Miss Mary's boxes to the center rail and Derry flattened out beside them.

"Here we go!" Tabs said, as he shoved off. "We're on our way."

It was a long cold sail. Longer and colder than any Derry had ever remembered. The wind was dead against them so that they were continuously going about for one short tack or another.

"We'll fly, going home," Derry said optimistically, but Tabs wasn't sure. He squinted up at the cold bleak sky and shrugged his shoulders. That was just the trouble with a day like this. The wind was coming due north right now, but it looked shifty.

They were nearly at the Knoll before Tabs enjoyed his sail at all. Then gradually he began to relax as much as he could in that dull, cramping cold. He looked up at the sail and it was well filled with wind. Tabs started to whistle, and just that second Derry let out a shout.

"Tabs!" she yelled. "Open water!"

For one dreadful instant Tabs was struck dumb. The next instant he shouted, "Hard alee!" Then he shot over his tiller with all his strength.

There was a flap of sails, the hiss of runners cutting the ice. The next instant the *Frost King* slid forward on still another tack. Tabs hunched down to look under the sail and saw where Derry was pointing.

There was open water all right. Yards of it, black and wind-rippled, and it looked even colder than the ice alongside. "Close!" said Tabs.

"Close!" Derry's clear blue eyes were frightened. "Tabs, it's terribly close! That gap stretches all the way from the Knoll right to the south side of the Beat. We can't go on this way. Not possibly."

Tabs measured the distance between himself and the dark curving outline of Blind Man's Beat and it seemed to grow longer every time he looked at it.

"There's still the marsh," he said. "That must be flooded after all this rain and it's on the north. Do you want to try it?"

For the first time that afternoon Derry grinned. "What do you think?" she said. "Do you think I want to go home and start knitting?"

Tabs grunted approval and once more barked the orders, "Ready about. Hard alee!"

They made the distance to the north side of Blind Man's Beat in fairly good time and then they saw the marshes in front of them. Most of the short stubble reeds were covered with good ice, but here and there clumps of brown stalks stood up like Indian top-knots. "It'll take sailing," Derry warned, peering under the sail. "You've got to give those clumps a wide berth."

Tabs had no time to talk. He took his line from the end of Blind Man's Beat and began sailing straight forward. Once he had to go about to escape a clump of reeds, and another time the ice creaked ominously beneath them. Still the *Frost King* moved steadily ahead.

They were nearly over the marsh when Tabs saw a last fringe of stubble between them and the clear ice near the shore.

"Tabs, look!" Derry warned, but now Tabs' mind was made up.

"Clear your sail," he ordered. "Get ready to take the tiller."

Somehow Derry forced her numb fingers to fasten the sail rope tightly around the brass cleat. At the same time Tabs edged farther and farther toward the stern of the little boat.

They drew near the fringe, nearer and nearer. There was no way of skirting it. "Now!" Tabs roared, and even as he spoke, Derry grabbed for the tiller.

At the same moment Tabs eased himself overboard. At the exact moment that the *Frost King's* bow hit the stubble, his feet hit the ice!

He shoved the boat forward with all his strength, shoved again, and then fell full length on the *Frost King's* stern just as she started to pull away from him!

For a moment Tabs could only lie face down on the wooden frame of the boat. Then slowly, gingerly, he pulled himself up. He saw that Derry still steered tensely for the point and that the stubble was several welcome yards behind them.

The ice was still thin. It groaned and creaked beneath them, but Tabs was not worried. They were near shore. A few shallow tacks and they would be alongside Miss Scarsborough's boathouse.

When they finally had the sails down and had

stepped on shore Tabs' knees shook and Derry was so cold her lips were blue. They unfastened Miss Mary's box from the *Frost King*'s center rail and lugged it onto the uneven beach. "Well," Derry said. "That was something. It's going to be even trickier going home."

"We can do it," Tabs said shortly and led the way up to Miss Scarsborough's big lonely house.

Miss Scarsborough was even gladder to see them than they had expected. When they gave her her groceries and magazines and Christmas cards, and their own package, Tabs was almost afraid she might be going to cry, but she didn't. Instead, she led them into her sitting room and put them close beside the lovely welcoming fire while she went out to get them some cocoa and send Robbie and Laddie in to get their own share of the Christmas box.

When Miss Mary came back with cocoa there were two small packages lying beside the white cups and the plate of cake. "For you," Miss Mary said, "and I like to open packages before Christmas."

Tabs grinned and opened his package while Miss Mary and Derry opened theirs. "Boy," Tabs got out, when the last piece of tissue paper was finally pulled away. "A compass, and what a beauty!"

He looked at Derry and saw that she had a stop watch. A really good stop watch, like the one Mr. Robinson used to start the boat races. Tabs looked

back at his own finely made compass and clicked down the lid with a little snap. "Boy," he said again, "these are wonderful."

"They're not nearly so nice as my dictionary," Miss Mary Scarsborough said, and it was plain that she really thought it. "Not nearly so nice, and I didn't deliver my presents."

Tabs smiled, and Derry pulled off her muffler as she moved even closer to the fire. "It was fun really," she told Miss Scarsborough. "Kind of exciting sometimes, but really fun."

Tabs and Derry could have stayed for hours, but they knew the short winter daylight was failing and they had to get home. Finally they pulled themselves away and stood by the arched doorway to say good-by. "And thanks an awful lot again for the presents," Derry began, but Miss Scarsborough stopped her with a little wave of the hand.

"They're nothing," she said, "nothing at all, but I thought they might be useful in your next races."

Tabs nodded, but as he pocketed his compass a little feeling of cold and disappointment shot through him. He and Derry wouldn't have any more races. At least not until the following summer in the catboat. As far as the All-Shrewsbury Iceboat Race was concerned, they were out.

They pulled on their mittens, waved to Miss Scarsborough, and charged down to the boathouse. The

Frost King was just where they had tied her, looking as old and forlorn as a battered scarecrow. Tabs began to pull up the sail, and for the first time he felt the new strength of the wind. "The wind's changed," Derry said. "It's going to be even more exciting going home."

It was exciting, but at least the excitement came at the beginning of the run. They headed for the marsh once, and then, as the wind failed, Tabs brought the *Frost King* sharply about. "We've got to wait for a real puff," Tabs said slowly. "And if it gives out just when we're halfway over, we're in trouble."

Derry edged gingerly toward the tiller, her eyes still ahead of her, searching for the best ice. Finally there was a sharp puff of wind. "All set?" Tabs asked, and Derry nodded.

The puff was a good one. It carried them safely over the flooded, frozen marsh and onto the black ice on the far side.

Then Tabs headed the *Frost King* down the long frozen channel toward the clubhouse. The wind was with them and if it didn't shift, they would soon be home.

The wind stayed favorable, and soon they were within sight of the clubhouse. Ben Van Bergh had lit a fire on the shore and Tabs and Derry could see two figures moving beside the leaping red flames.

"Home free!" Derry said, as they slid over the

rough ice of the harbor. "Home free and nobody took an ice bath."

Tabs nodded, one hand on his tiller and one hand on his pocket, where he could feel the bulge of the compass. He turned the *Frost King* skillfully windward and in another moment they had the sail down and were taking it off.

Ben helped them lift the boat up on blocks. Then the twins realized that Mr. Robinson was the other figure they had seen. "Well," he said, "you people go out on any sort of ice. How far did you get to?"

"Up to Blind Man's Beat," Tabs said quietly, and then Derry told him how they had nearly ended up in the open water on the south side.

"How'd you finally manage?" Mr. Robinson asked, and his eyes, in the red firelight, were alive with interest.

"Over the marsh," Derry told him. "Tabs knew it would be flooded and we were pretty sure it would be frozen."

Mr. Robinson led the way inside the warm clubhouse. "You people know your river," he said. "How would you like to go in the All-Shrewsbury Race?"

For once Tabs spoke before Derry. "Like it?" he said. "We'd like it better than anything in the world, but the *Frost King* came in last on the trial race."

Mr. Robinson dismissed the *Frost King* with one shrug of his broad shoulders. "I didn't mean that," he said. "I meant, how would you like to come along as my crew on board the *Snow Queen?* I'm looking for someone who knows the river."

A few minutes later the twins marched up the hill toward home. They were still cold but they walked briskly, as befitted the crew of the best iceboat on the river.

"What a piece of luck!" Derry was saying as they got near their own house. "And all just because we went to see Miss Mary. You'd think we'd really done something, the way he talked."

Tabs patted the pocket that held his new compass. "I'll take this along as a good-luck piece in the All-Shrewsbury," he said.

"To remind you of the Christmas-Present Race!" laughed Derry. "And of the good little *Frost King* that won it."